AF264721

Stephen was born in 1957 in Beverley East Yorkshire and whilst his parents Jean and Tony Dobbs were ecstatically happy his elder brother Kevan wasn't. He wanted a rabbit.

He grew up in the seaside town of Hornsea where his father worked at the local pottery (as did he) mother was a housewife. He has two brothers on younger and one older and with a freshwater lake close by and the north sea around the corner, the holderness countryside as well, insipation was not a problem for him. He has worked abroad for a short time as well. Many thanks

To Christopher and Kevan in equal measure

Stephen James Dobbs

EVACUATION

AUSTIN MACAULEY PUBLISHERS®

LONDON * CAMBRIDGE * NEW YORK * SHARJAH

Copyright © Stephen James Dobbs 2024

The right of Stephen James Dobbs to be identified as author of this work has been asserted by the author in accordance with sections 77 and 78 of the Copyright, Designs and Patents Act 1988.

All rights reserved. No part of this publication may be reproduced, stored in a retrieval system, or transmitted in any form or by any means, electronic, mechanical, photocopying, recording, or otherwise, without the prior permission of the publishers.

Any person who commits any unauthorised act in relation to this publication may be liable to criminal prosecution and civil claims for damages.

This is a work of fiction. Names, characters, businesses, places, events, locales, and incidents are either the products of the author's imagination or used in a fictitious manner. Any resemblance to actual persons, living or dead, or actual events is purely coincidental.

A CIP catalogue record for this title is available from the British Library.

ISBN 9781035847600 (Paperback)
ISBN 9781035847617 (ePub e-book)

www.austinmacauley.com

First Published 2024
Austin Macauley Publishers Ltd®
1 Canada Square
Canary Wharf
London
E14 5AA

Prologue

The alien spacecraft approaching Earth slowed considerably, before arcing to begin an entry-orbit, glowing fiercely white-hot as friction acted upon its disc-like exterior.

A few moments later, the silver-dose pulled free of resistance and entered the planet's atmosphere, finding itself easily able to power through its upper air at will.

"What speed is it doing?"

Colonel Christopher Smithlington wanted to know as he stood staring unsmilingly up at the enormous main wall viewing-screen in front of him in control headquarters.

"Mach-eight! Mach-seven! Mach-six! It's definitely slowing down…"

Drawled flight-technician Perry Goldbright, the person responsible for data confirming target speed and altitude at command centre HQ.

"Where exactly is it and what are its headings?"

Barked the furrow-browed colonel without removing his gaze from the hugely elongated screen as the glowing blip raced across unbelievably fast yet slowing as it went.

"It's currently in British airspace heading north-east!" Another of his trusted team of technicians in the rapid-response unit, Roy Kingcrave, informed, treble-checking the statistics on his monitor as he did so.

"I assume that it is well above civilian aircraft flight-paths; if so, any guesses as to its final destination?"

"Yes, Colonel, it's presently five miles up but descending at a rapid rate of one-mile per fifty, my guess would be somewhere in Scandinavia," volunteered flight-technician, Sally Pondersby, from the console, immediately to his right; her informed opinion was the same as his, hardly surprising seeing as she was his own daughter.

"How long till interception and where will it take place?" Colonel Smithlington quizzed whilst mentally digesting the many items of information appearing across the gigantic screen via the individual computer consoles feeding it.

"Fighters have been scrambled from the nearest air force base to us and they are due to intercept it in four minutes over the east coast of Yorkshire," revealed a confident-sounding Sally Pondersby a question of her own suddenly desperate to be both heard and answered as the blip continued onwards across the giant screen.

"Colonel Smithlington, are you intending to try and shoot that spacecraft down in one piece or destroy it completely?"

"We want it in one piece of course, but the fates may intervene and cost us the main prize, but at least we will still have what is in the wreckage," replied the officer-in-charge of the team of technicians there. "Not to mention being responsible for the capture of the UFO if at all possible. Speaking of which, see if you can set up a two-way intercom communication between us and the lead pilot; clear it with RAF area command, will you, Sally."

"Two minutes to intercept, Colonel," droned John Brainwest from the very end console, his high-pitched voice cutting through all and any complacency around the control room as strike time drew nearer.

The moment he finished speaking, another voice filled the air waves as the lead pilot reached the designated rendezvous place, his words silencing the control room as one.

"Flight headquarters, I have a visual on the bogie, I repeat I have a visual on the bogie, request permission to commence attack manoeuvre."

"It's a 'green-for-go', Zero-Tango-Tango, try to bring it down with minimum damage; over," advised an unsmiling Colonel Smithlington, the officer-in-charge, deliberately cutting off area command with instructions of his own as to how to conduct the mission.

"Roger that, there it is in my sights, it's unmissable, almost as if daring me to strike. Here goes…"

They heard the pilot confirm the order only for the airwaves to suddenly go static-free, ominously so, bringing a sense of fear and foreboding as events unfolded.

"Zero-Tango-Tango, come in? What's happening up there? Can you hear me, Zero-Tango-Tango?" An agonised Colonel Smithlington quizzed as the sudden deafening silence brought looks of anguish to the faces of everyone sitting listening on.

"For God's sake, answer me! This has to be a communication blackout, it can't be anything else. Zero-Tango-Tango, speak to me, come in, that's if you haven't been shot down yourself!"

"I got him! Not quite a direct hit because it took evasive measures at the very last moment, my guess is that it didn't see me until then."

"YES!" A momentarily unprofessional Colonel Smithlington blurted as news of the mission's seeming success hit home, much to the amusement of his team looking and listening on.

"Erm…I mean say again, confirm hit along with your location, status and situation; over."

"Yes, Sir. I'm currently near the east, over a seaside town called Hornsea. The bogie is going down at quite a steep rate towards what appears to be a large body of freshwater," Informed the victorious pilot whilst keeping one eye on the stricken alien spacecraft and the other on his own panel of instruments.

"I thought as much. Yes, he is definitely going to ditch into the lake down there; conditions are perfect for it seeing as it's very dark and cloudy out on the coast at this time of night."

"Well done, Zero-Tango-Tango, return to base. We'll take it from here via radar sweep. Over and out."

"Roger that and good luck; out."

With the pilot's words ringing in his ears, Colonel Smithlington turned to face his team of technicians who sat checking readings on their various consoles.

"Right, people, listen carefully. We are going to set up a round-the-clock twenty-four-seven radar surveillance on that lake out on the east coast," enthused the confident-sounding colonel, knowing as he did that he and his team had done the hard bit and managed to down a UFO in the first instance.

"Then, we are going to have to come up with a credible reason for dredging that body of water, One that will not arouse any suspicion amongst the local population. Well, any ideas?"

"Yes, I think that I might have the solution. Why don't we have the entire town evacuated on some pretext or other?" A usually dependant Sally proffered as the others listened in stunned silence; even the colonel seemed stoney-faced at first. Then he warmed to the idea.

"Interesting! Interesting, but what could we propose that could possibly cause a mass evacuation?"

It was Sally who once again came up with the goods, her idea, whilst sounding completely off the radar was quite plausible; in fact, he liked it; he liked it a lot.

Chapter One

For twelve year old John Philips, the beginning of very much welcomed summer holidays spent away from boarding school was to have a perfect start. It didn't, anything but...

Instead of being met at the train station when he finally made it to the city of Hull, he found himself standing there all alone, his parents nowhere to be seen.

All he could think of to do was stand close to the row of red telephone kiosks and await a call from them whilst peering in all directions just in case.

What on Earth could have happened to them? mused the frowning boy to himself. Surely they had gotten his letter telling them that it was school holidays at long last...

He posted the letter at least ten days ago, asking that his two parents meet his train as per usual; yet here he was standing by himself in the busy station alone.

He had spent what little money he had on train fares so he could not get the bus or a minicab; there was nothing else for it. He'd just have to walk there, that's all.

There was nothing to it. It may be fourteen miles away but he and some pals had done it once before, albeit the other way around, and gotten a lift part way there as well.

Why not? It was a nice warm sunny afternoon, perfect for what was an adventurous journey out to the east coast and he might just hitch a ride somewhere along the way.

There had to be a very good reason as to why his mother and father were not there to meet and greet him. Had they crashed? Had the car been stolen? What happened?

Whatever it was, he'd only find out by getting home and asking them that question. With that in mind, he turned and headed for the exit.

Then he remembered the time he called directory enquiries and got them to connect him to the telephone in Hornsea and get his parents to accept and pay for the call.

With that in mind, John turned on his heels and strode back into the busy railway station making a beeline for the bank of phone kiosks to do just that.

All were occupied except one and that was where he went, only to quickly discover why it stank of both urine and cigar smoke mixed with something he couldn't quite recognise.

The vile stench made him gag and very nearly vomit but he kept both his nerve and delicious breakfast as he picked up the receiver and dialled the directory enquiries' people.

Miracle of miracles, he managed to get his call connected only for it to ring and ring and ring. Clearly, they were not there, but where were they both?

That question and its answer would just have to wait thought the boy and was suddenly desperate to begin the long journey to the east coast and home.

Turning on his heels, John again headed for the exit, this time walking purposefully in the general direction he knew Hornsea and the east coast to be.

His plans to hitch a ride did not materialise, at least not at first as he followed the busy main road dual carriageway through the city centre thumbing occasionally but with no success.

Eventually, someone did stop a couple of miles out of the city itself when a lorry driver took pity on him, pulling to a noisy break, squealing halt just ahead of him.

Once the relieved boy revealed his destination, the grinning driver offered to drop him off at the nearest turn-off to it seeing as how he was heading for the port of Bridlington.

John thanked him as they continued onwards out of Hull on the ever-busy coast road between the former and Bridlington, a sudden foul smell filling his nostrils as they went.

"You're carrying pigs, aren't you?"

"Yes, I am. I bet you can't guess how many bacon sandwiches you could make even if I were to tell you exactly how many are back there, eh sunshine?" The muscular driver responded with a quite theatrical wink, one that instantly set the scene for what was a friendly ambience. His host continued.

"By the way, what's your name or shall I keep calling you 'sunshine'?"

"I'm John, John Philips, and no, I can't even begin to guess how many bacon sandwiches; thanks," replied an unsmiling John Philips; right one to keep what he thought to himself, the stench from the live cargo behind infiltrating into the cab even though the driver's window was wound down.

"Well, John, my name's Rob. How come you are travelling alone? Where are your parents?"

"I…I have begun my summer holidays from boarding school but my parents were not at the station to meet me. I did write to tell them honestly," warbled the furrow-browed boy with a scowl of disappointment, one noted by his host behind the wheels of the lorry they were travelling along the road in.

"I'm sorry to hear that, young John. Will they be waiting for you when you get to where you're going?"

A concerned Rob wanted to know whilst overtaking a trio of cars, all three seemingly stuck in first gear making him beep his horn in response to their joint slowness.

"I hope so, then again, we might pass them on their way through to meet me in Hull. I don't think so anyhow," replied the thoughtful boy as once again Rob threw the vehicle into the outside lane to overtake a much slower car before going back over to the inside again.

"I hope so as well, young John. Are you hungry at all, because if you are, then I may have a couple of sandwiches in my bag," proffered the happy-go-lucky driver with a smile. His enquiry reminded John that he had not eaten since breakfast early that same morning and he was extremely peckish.

"Well, actually, I am feeling quite hungry but I don't want to be a nuisance at all."

"Hey, you're not a nuisance. Help yourself, reach over and grab the sandwich box from my bag; go on, young man."

A reluctant John did just that, rummaging around in the driver's holdall until he located his lunch box, then flipped up the lid and looked inside.

Several thick-cut sandwiches nestled beside an over-ripe pear and seeing as he hated most fruits, he plumped for one of the former, lifting one out then replaced the plastic lid.

"Thanks, what's in it please?"

"Sardine and peanut butter. I know it sounds awful but believe me, they are fantastic. Go on, give it a go," urged the smiling driver, watching with curiosity at first as the uncertain boy took a tentative bite and began chewing. His face quickly changed as he started to enjoy what he was eating.

"I told you that it was nice. Eat the others if you like, there's a cafe I know in Bridlington, I'll have something there," crowed a grinning Rob, quite enjoying watching the boy's expression flip from uncertain over to definitely interested as he chewed away.

"You might as well take them with you because we are only a mile or so from the turn you want. I'm only sorry that I can't take you all the way but this lorry is on a tachograph."

"Hmm, you're right, they are very nice. I will take the other if it's alright with you."

John informed him by way of reply; the twelve year old boy was quite looking forward to giving the recipe to his mother so that she could make him some in the future.

"Here's your turning just up ahead, grab that other sarnie and I'll pull over whilst you climb out and down, yes?" His kindly host was enthused as the pig-carrying lorry began slowing prior to stopping to allow John to exit, which he did, grabbing the remaining sandwich as well as his own bag.

Once out, John could only stand on the grass verge waving as the lorry full of pigs drove away and was soon around the corner and out of sight.

Crossing the busy coast road, he started walking along the road he knew would be reasonably free of traffic with only occasional vehicles to cadge a lift with.

A couple of miles into the journey, a car pulled to the side of the road and a woman's voice asked if he wanted a lift at all. He did; thanking her as he climbed into the front passenger seat.

"And what might your name be, young fellow?" A fairly large, flinty-haired woman enquired. In tones, John found reminiscent of one of his teachers back at the boarding school. She was a bit of a dragon as well.

"John Philips. I'm on my way to meet my parents in Hornsea. I am on holiday from boarding school but mum and dad didn't meet me up at the railway station at Hull," rattled off an unphased John as the piggy-eyed woman stared at him for a moment as if he was stupid or something, then she spoke.

"You obviously haven't heard the news then. Hornsea has been evacuated. Apparently, they discovered an atom bomb that was dumped in the Mere back in the nineteen fifties!"

The matronly woman informed him matter of factly. The news that his own quiet little seaside resort had a nuclear bomb there was mad. Was she joking? Then she continued.

"Oh, not a big one but they reckoned it would be enough to destroy most of the town. All animals as well from pets to the cows and horses in the surrounding fields were driven away."

"Atomic bomb! Hey, it's not April Fool's day, is it, Missus, erm…I don't know your name, do I?" The quizzical boy exclaimed, his face a mask of disbelieve and incredulity at her statement. Surely she was joking about it all. Hornsea and atom bombs were an impossible combination.

"It's Missus Higginbottom and I'm not in the habit of telling lies, young man. You can ask anyone in Sigglesthorne and they will tell you just that," bustled the scowling woman. Driving the car, her expression was one of possible violence and ejection if he wasn't careful. He had to apologise to her if he didn't want to walk.

"Not that you meant to be offensive, I know that, but you will not manage to get into Hornsea at all. The entire town is sealed off and heavily guarded as well."

"Heavily guarded? If there is really a bomb and it goes off, then there won't be anything left to protect, will there?" The head strong boy quizzed with a concerned frown on his face in reaction to the news that the seaside resort was a no-entry zone as far as the outside world was concerned.

"I think it's more to do with stopping people from the outside breaking into shops and other properties than anything else," corrected his unsmiling hostess as they drove ever nearer to the town in question. Three miles to Hornsea read a road sign but it was the one above it that caught his attention.

'Hornsea closed to all persons; extreme danger, armed patrols will fire live ammunition; keep out, you have been warned.'

"Besides, the experts will soon find and disarm the bomb, then all will be back to normal there."

"I hope so, but what if my parents are still there waiting for me to turn up, what then?" John uttered with slightly flagging confidence as the car started slowing down, the woman behind the wheel pulling to a halt at the grass verge as several vehicles overtook them.

"Well, here we are, young master John. This is where I turn off for Sigglesthorne. I suggest that you find a telephone box and call your parents," advised his seriously overweight hostess as he climbed out of the car and closed the door behind him. Victoria Higginbottom rolled the passenger side window down to finish her sentence.

"I'd stay well away from Hornsea if I were you, it isn't safe. Still, I suppose 'boys will be boys'. Goodbye and good luck."

"Yes, and thanks for the lift, Missus Higginbottom. Goodbye."

On saying that, the smiling woman rewound the window and then drove away, leaving him still three miles from his destination. It was then that he began to have second thoughts.

Was he doing the right thing? Should he risk his life going to Hornsea or would he be wise to keep his distance? Perhaps he was making a very big mistake after all…

As the two miles to go sign loomed in the distance, he had made his mind up to continue on to the now deserted seaside resort and see what was going on for himself.

Half a mile further on, another sign caught his attention. This one was an even stronger warning that under no circumstances were any persons to even attempt to enter Hornsea, if so, they would be held and prosecuted for criminal trespass.

He had just gone a few steps past the sign when an army jeep drove past, slowing to a halt, then reversing back, the driver was anxious to speak with him.

"I take it that you have read that sign back there. Where are you going, young man?" A stern-faced soldier wanted to know, his expression scaring the boy at first as he stared at the man addressing him. John lost his nerve as well as his voice momentarily.

"I…I…I'm heading home to erm…Hatfield. How about giving me a lift if it's alright to do so?" He heard himself say, being deliberately cheeky to the soldier in order to avoid him guessing anything to the contrary and stopping him from going any further.

"Alright then, jump in and I'll take you there myself," agreed the man behind the wheel with a toothy grin. John doing just that, opened the door and climbed in before closing it again as the jeep set off.

"Is it alright to ask you a question?" John asked as they began the relatively short journey; the nervy boy unsure as to whether it would be against the army rules to reveal anything at all to someone not in uniform.

"Yes, of course, you can as long as it doesn't force me to break the Official Secrets Act, fire away."

"Where did that atomic bomb in Hornsea Mere come from? Was it dropped by the Germans during World War Two?"

It was a good question and one the knowledgeable soldier was only too eager and able to answer; after all, what harm could it do to tell a young boy like him?

"No, the Germans did not possess an atomic bomb thank God. If they did, they would probably have used it on this country and across Europe as well," rattled off his uniform-wearing host as they drove ever closer to the tiny village of Hatfield, the soldier revealing exactly what he knew to be true.

"No, this one is one of our own experiments in low-grade, very compact atomic devices; one accidentally lost some time in the late nineteen fifties."

"One of our own? Supposing it had gone off back then, it would have killed my grandparents and I might not have been born at all?"

"Hell! How old did you say you were?" A shocked yet impressed private, Steven Henderson, quizzed; the furrow-browed soldier having not expected such deep thinking from such a very young boy.

"Twelve; thirteen next month."

John was pleased and proud to announce to his seemingly stunned host, the young boy having been taught about such things that same year back in school.

"Did you now. Well, it didn't go off and here you are. Next stop, Hatfield."

True to his word, there followed a road sign saying just that they had arrived at the village of Hatfield and John knew the area only too well.

"Erm, you can drop me anywhere around here, I'll walk the rest of the way," bluffed the semi-confident boy. As they entered the tiny village, John suddenly was anxious to be rid of his army host and take stock of the situation.

"Okay, Mister Philips, you are safe enough here, but if I were you, I wouldn't go any nearer to the coast, not until you hear on the news that it is safe to do so," warned the knowledgeable soldier with a wink as he pulled the jeep to a halt just past the water tower and turned to face the eager to be away boy sat beside him.

"Give my regards to your parents and be lucky in life. So long, son."

"Yes, I will do that, and thanks. I hear that they will shoot to kill if they catch anyone breaking into shops or houses. Have the army got tanks there as well?"

"No need for a tank. There are armed patrols every ten minutes as well as a helicopter using ultraviolet heat sensitive search and identify equipment," droned the clearly well-informed army private in all seriousness; his expression one of parental sternness as he informed the blank-faced boy sat listening on.

"There is also a radar sweep around the clock seawards just in case anyone tries to land and come ashore. All in all, security is extremely effective."

"Don't worry about me, I'm going home to my mum and dad. Thanks for the lift," John told him prior to climbing off the jeep and closing the door behind him, strolling casually away as the soldier drove on towards Hornsea.

What to do for the best? mused the confident boy as he stopped and took stock of his situation. He had come this far, why not go all the way; it made perfect sense to him.

With that thought in mind, he turned and walked in the direction of the departed army jeep. As he did so, a sudden thought flitted through his mind, one he needed to address.

According to the soldier, he wouldn't be allowed to simply walk in Hornsea. It would require skill and cunning for him to sneak into there without being seen.

If that was the case, he was on the wrong road. If he was going to successfully outmanoeuvre the security people surrounding it, he needed to enter from the north.

Cutting across the country was easy for him seeing as he knew the area like the back of his hand. John used the main road to begin with then the back doubles.

Two miles and half a dozen fields later, he reached the town's most northerly route. Into it, Seaton road led down a long sloping gradient in a straight line for well over a mile in length.

With Hornsea under martial law, even though it had been ordered to be evacuated, the resort would still have at least a half-mile exclusion zone around it.

The knowledgeable boy knew full well that he would not be able to enter his hometown by road but where though. He did know a few ways into Hornsea but they were still further up ahead.

He was about half a mile from the town itself when he heard it. It could only be the sound of helicopter rotor blades and they were getting closer with each passing second.

There had to be somewhere to hide but where? screamed part of the young boy's suddenly desperate mind as he looked around him for a place to dive into.

On an impulse, he turned to his right and quickly vaulted over a high wooden fence landing on the edge of a field of cabbages that were huge-leaved and ready to be picked.

Without a moment's thought, he began running as hard as he could, keeping to thick hedgerow along the southern border as the sound of approaching helicopter blades grew ever louder.

There was a deeply wooded area at the far end of the field which would be the ideal place to hide from the helicopters with ultraviolet heat-seeking equipment.

There was a way into the forest and he might just make it to safety after all, mused the sprinting boy, only to lose his footing and fall face-first onto a big fat cabbage with only a few yards to go.

Fate had dealt him a savage blow as he bounced off the cabbage and lay still gasping for breath, the wind knocked from his lungs just as the helicopter came into view.

All was lost, or was it? thought the breathless boy noticing a length of half-buried long-discarded pipe left behind when the field's irrigation system was installed.

With seconds to spare, John scrambled furiously over to it and crawled straight in ignoring the enormous spider's web stretched across the entrance.

John could only lay statue still and listen as the helicopter flew this way and that overhead whilst the startled arachnid ran for cover, it's home now in tatters.

From his new found hiding place in the damp-smelling pipe, he could hear but not see the thrumming helicopter blades as it flew over the field of cabbages.

It didn't take very long before he heard it begin to diminish. John caught sight of it as it flew away to continue on its prearranged course around Hornsea.

Only when he saw it disappear from view altogether did he crawl from the filthy pipe and stand staring out in the direction it had taken.

The disgustingly cramped pipe had protected him from those in the helicopter by shielding his body heat from the ultraviolet device they were using.

It had worked out for him this time but would he be so lucky the next time it happened? That would have to sort itself out if and when it took place.

Now though he had to make his way into the woodlands before the helicopter came back again, which it undoubtedly would sooner or later.

A moment later, he was strolling into the copse of dense trees he knew reasonably well, having played out in and around the town all his young life and these woods in particular.

Once under the canopy of trees, he was safe from detection at least from the air; hopefully, there were no police or soldiers in there as well.

He needn't have worried; the woods were empty as usual, save for an abundance of wildlife and birds twittering merrily away up in the thickly matted canopy overhead.

John knew the right track to take and quickly made his way to the opposite side of the woodlands. His hay fever kicked in, making him sneeze furiously as he went along.

The trail he had taken brought him out behind a set of garages and that's where he stayed, red eyes streaming whilst the sneezes finally slowed and then stopped altogether.

It took a few minutes before he was back to normal again and ready to continue, having decided that staying hidden and off the main roads was all important in the circumstances.

Leaving the relative safety of the garages, he strolled gingerly around the corner and out into the familiar side road, looking and listening every step of the way.

With blood pounding in his ears, the wary child began a steady stroll knowing full well that he would have to cross the main road in a few moments' time.

The town was deathly quiet as opposed to its usual hustle and bustle of cars, lorries, and especially people; now only birds sang occasionally but nothing else.

A couple of turns further on brought him out very close to the normally busy main road out of Hornsea going west; now though it was devoid of any and all traffic whatsoever.

Again, he remained statue still and listened, hearing and seeing nothing at all; no people chatting away as normally would but more importantly, no traffic.

With the latter in mind, he braced himself and then began sprinting as fast as he could for the other side, stopping the moment he reached the road opposite and then stood listening.

Thankfully, no vehicles or people sounded around the corner it seemed that his luck was in, then he heard a noise he had come to recognise and filled him with dread.

It was the rotor blades of the search helicopter constantly circling the evacuated resort, making sure that no one had entered the town to loot and steal.

Remembering the technology they were using, he needed to find a suitable hiding place, one that would shield him from detection by the helicopter's heat-seeking apparatus. But where?

He had just two choices—he could run back into the woods and hide there but that was too far away, he'd never make it there in time, they would track his heat image.

On the other hand, there would be no point in his hiding in a doorway, they'd soon find him. There didn't seem to be anywhere and the helicopter was almost upon him.

Then he saw the possible answer to his prayers—a common or garden dustbin—hopefully, empty enough for him to climb into. If not, he'd be in very deep trouble indeed.

Breaking into a run, he sprinted hard for the bins, reaching them in a breathless panic as rotor blades filled his ears. He yanked off the lid only to find it nearly full of rubbish.

The one beside it was, thankfully, almost empty and in desperation, he began clambering inside. John was oblivious to the smell such was his determination to evade capture.

With pulse pounding in his ears along with the helicopter's rotor blades almost overhead, he slumped down in the thin metal casing and pulled the lid hurriedly into place.

Just as the metal lid slid into position, he caught sight of the search helicopter going slowly over the house top whose dustbin he had chosen to hide in.

Whilst he was safe from possible detection, he was far from safe from choking to death such was the almost overpowering stench he had lowered himself down into.

It was so bad that it made the young boy cough and retch with such spasmodic violence that at one point, he almost managed to overturn the stinking dustbin altogether.

That was the very last thing he needed to happen in the present circumstances seeing as how he would be instantly noticed by the crew aboard the hovering helicopter.

As luck would have it, the helicopter had long since departed by the time he came up for air. John gulped the fresh air into his lungs whilst climbing out of the foul-smelling bin.

With the danger nowhere in sight, he replaced the lid on the bin and listened, hearing only his blood pounding in both ears but no helicopter anywhere. He was safe for now.

With that thought in mind, he began a slow jog down the ghostly quiet side road towards the town's enormous freshwater lake known locally as the 'Mere'.

Hornsea Mere was the largest lake in Yorkshire and a popular tourist attraction to those visiting the seaside resort, not to mention locals old and young.

Apart from its row boat and tourist boat facilities, it also boasted unrivalled yacht racing, not to mention superb fishing for huge pike and other freshwater fishes.

No one in Hornsea knew more about the Mere and surrounding countryside than he did, even fewer knew the way across the adjoining fields so as to bypass the main road altogether.

It did, however, mean that he would be easily and openly seen by anyone observing those fields, especially the helicopter, should it take that particular route.

It was a risk he was going to have to take bearing in mind the field's lack of horses and occasional clumps of head-high reeds to hide behind as he went.

There was no doubt about it; Hornsea was now a veritable 'ghost town' with no people or vehicles whatsoever in sight; quite disturbing to a local like him.

The risk was well worth the effort if it meant staying off the main roads and away from prying eyes. Having come this far the last thing he needed was to get himself caught.

The fields in question lay around a fairly wide stretch of open road known as the Mere-side; it was at the rear of the resort's normally quite busy town centre market place.

The road itself ran for two hundred metres or so before turning right for another hundred metres to the fields themselves. It was dotted with places to hide but not from a helicopter.

With confidence running fifty-fifty with caution, he stepped out and began a brisk walk keeping wherever possible to the walls and hedges, all the while fully alert to any movements around him.

So far so good, he told himself on reaching the gentle right-hand turn and caught sight of his goal up ahead, tentatively keeping to the side of a block of two-storey flats as he went.

He was barely twenty metres from the field when the sound of a car engine made him stop dead in his tracks, dodging behind an enormous privet hedge and kneeling down as he did so.

As he knelt peering out between the dark green leaves, two cars drove from left to right at the T junction up ahead, heading he knew to the shores of the giant freshwater lake around the next corner.

Luckily for him, he had not been noticed at all by those inside either vehicle as they raced by, if he had not ducked down they would definitely have seen him.

Having successfully dodged the cars and with no helicopter in sight or hearing range, his confidence suddenly grew wings as he stood up and headed for the first field.

It would prove fantastic fun having Hornsea all to himself John mused as he reached, then quickly vaulted the wooden gate, finding it strange with no horses anywhere around him.

The only danger involved in the cross fields route was a rather awkward crossing of the Mere's overflow lock gates, a manoeuvre he had done successfully before on many occasions.

About half way across the field, he stopped hearing raised voices coming from the direction of the Mere-side itself, forcing him to sidle into a big clump of tall reeds just in case.

Had they seen him or were they simply conversing a little bit louder than he imagined they would? No judging from their tones as they were yelling occasional orders. He was still quite safe.

He could hear them talking but not actually see what they were doing. The only way to do that was to get to the lock gates and peer across the lake from there.

With that thought in mind, he continued onwards, remembering to stick as closely as possible to whatever natural cover was there to avoid detection.

The one thing he had not reasoned for was that whilst there were no more horses, he had not counted on stepping in their piles of droppings still scattered like land mines around the field.

Having slid awkwardly on one clump of soft-smelling coconuts, he made damn sure that it did not happen again.

John quickly discovered that whilst the busy Mere landing area and boathouse were well shielded by a wide clump of trees and bushes, it soon turned into flat open land.

The closer he got to the overflow lock gates, the less cover was available to dodge into and hide behind, making him more visible should anyone be gazing in his direction.

As he had expected, the bushes and trees ended leaving him quite a distance to go with hardly any cover at all, John putting his head down and sprinting as hard as he could.

On reaching the lock gates, the desperate boy dived for cover, settling down behind a foot-high grassy mound put there deliberately in case of unwanted overflows into the surrounding fields.

With heart pounding in his chest, he raised his head and peered tentatively over the top of the grassy mound, realising with a relieved sigh that he had not been seen and alarms raised.

He had an undisturbed view of activities across the wind-whipped waters between him and the work going on over at the busy boathouse and yacht-lined peninsula beyond.

From what he could see, it was a real hive of activity with lots of men wandering around wearing white boiler suits and meandering into and out of an array of apparatus and porta cabins.

One or two were wearing space suits whilst manipulating various devices on the yacht and row boat lined bank and frogmen dived to and from a vessel out on the lake itself.

The space suits he could well understand what with radiation a very real possibility following a nuclear bomb going off but why not everyone else over there as well? Then he heard it, rotor blades from the oncoming search helicopter.

The sound of approaching helicopter rotor blades forced him to turn and anxiously seek out a hiding place. Seeing nothing anywhere in sight, then he remembered the pipe.

The pipe itself carried any and all released freshwater away into a stream dyke and from there out into the nearby North Sea and would be an ideal place to hide in.

It may well be the perfect hiding place but in his eagerness to do so, he had forgotten all about the solid wire grill there to stop birds nesting inside or other animals making it their home.

With the helicopter getting ever closer, John peered around for an alternative place to hide but had to admit that it was the partially overgrown pipe or nothing.

With that in mind and the helicopter almost upon him, John made a lunge for the uninviting pipe outlet, still trying to remember if there was a way to remove the wire grill.

The approaching helicopter was attracting the attention of one or two white boiler-suited men over at the Mere-side peninsula but he gritted his teeth and worked on the problem.

He remembered at the same moment that the helicopter came into view out and over the choppy waters of the Mere as he gripped the grime-encrusted mesh and pulled hard down on it.

With more luck than he deserved, the entire top half peeled away with a loud yet satisfying squeal, leaving just enough room for him to clamber backwards into the unsavoury interior.

Half expecting to be hailed loudly through an external megaphone from the search helicopter at any moment, he tugged the grill back into place as the chopper circled to face him.

With seconds to spare, the desperate boy launched himself bodily backwards, scrambling and kicking for extra purchase deeper into the stinking depths of the overflow pipe.

Having slid himself ten or twelve feet, he stopped and listened, hearing the helicopter's rotor blades hovering very close by but not trying to land with any luck.

All he could do was stay there until the helicopter flew away. How long that could be was anyone's guess but at least it would allow him time to think about certain things.

The interior of his newly found hiding place stank to high heaven and was extremely damp. John found himself sitting in a disgusting inch or so of stagnant water but at least he was out of sight and reasonably safe.

A series of distant squeals and rustlings emanating from behind him somewhere in the deep pipeline made the scared boy shiver but his thoughts were on events going on outside instead.

Despite the possible dangers from whatever was making all the scrapings and scurrying sounds, he could not afford to panic and hurriedly exit the pipe, not yet anyway.

For a full five minutes, he sat in the unlit overflow pipe heart in mouth staring at the cobweb and slime-covered wire grill, not knowing what was going on outside.

For all he knew, they were even now running for the lock gates to pull him from the pipe, the helicopter about to land in the empty field to flush him out of hiding.

With that thought going through his mind, John remained where he was, fear of discovery furrowing his forehead but in the end, he knew that he could not stay there indefinitely.

With heart pounding away in his chest, he began a slow sequence of lurches ever closer to the filthy outer grill, all the time looking and listening for any unusual sounds or movements.

Once at the grill itself, he was able to see and hear what was happening. The nervous boy quickly realised that there was no helicopter anywhere to be either seen or heard.

By carefully pushing open the filthy metal grill, he could see across to the Mere-side peninsula noticing straight away that the work was continuing as normal. He had not been seen.

Forgetting whatever was scurrying around further down the evil-smelling overflow pipe, it was time to leave. John forced open the rusted grill and eased himself out into the fresh air.

Once out, he turned and replaced the mesh grill to its original position so as not to arouse suspicion; the last thing he wanted was to announce his presence in the town.

A quick look around told him that the helicopter had gone and he could continue his journey home, keeping low as he began a staggered run across the much smaller second field along.

Luckily for him, he reached the safety of the trees without being noticed and stood peering back in the direction of the busy Mere-view peninsula directly over the water from him.

It was the same hive of activity as always with lots of people in white boiler suits strolling around doing things; now all he had to do was dodge the helicopter again and he'd make it home.

With that thought in mind, John turned and clambered his way over a low wooden fence finding himself on a familiar elbow cul de sac leading to the main road close to his home address.

On reaching the main Hull road, John stood listening, hoping for his own sake that the ever-present helicopter would not be in the area, which thankfully it was not.

He was halfway across the main road when he heard the sounds of distant rotor blades growing ever louder, the search helicopter was heading his way and would soon be upon him.

He needed a place to hide but where? Should he double back and find somewhere down the alley? No, it was too far to run, there had to be another place. But where?

All he could see around him for shelter were nearby gardens and the red telephone box standing on the very corner of the T junction itself, it was one or the other, but which?

With the dreaded helicopter getting ominously closer, he plummeted for the telephone box, running and reaching it with seconds to spare as loud rotor blades sounded close by.

He grabbed the metal handle and pulled at the door forgetting just how stiff and heavy it was to open, but fear of being discovered gave him strength he never knew he possessed.

The moment John entered the box, he caught sight of the helicopter flying low over the trees towards him. It was enough to force him down onto his hands and knees on the cold concrete floor.

All he could again do was remain perfectly still and not move a single muscle, which was exactly what he did,

Extremely loud rotor blades told the cowering boy that the grey helicopter was hovering almost directly overhead. His body heat was hopefully masked by the roof of the claustrophobic kiosk.

Nerves once again jangled as he knelt at the foot of a litter-strewn, foul-smelling telephone box awaiting the departure of the annoying search helicopter.

He didn't have too long to wait before the grey helicopter flew slowly away from there presumably in the direction of the town centre, though he could not tell.

Once all was quiet, John risked a quick look outside, peering cautiously out through one dirty oblong window and then another direction until satisfied that the coast was clear and it was safe to carry on.

Pushing the heavy door fully open, he stood breathing in the welcomed fresh air knowing as he did that home was well within reach now that the danger had past.

Setting off with a cocky confident stride, he rounded the corner and entered the council estate he knew and loved, reminding himself that stealth was necessary all the same.

He needn't have worried as he reached Trinity Road without any sight or sound of the ubiquitous helicopter. His home had never looked so good or as welcoming as it did there and then.

The moment John turned and began the short walk down the path between adjoining council houses, he realised that his parents would have undoubtedly locked the outer passage door.

It was not like his mum and dad not to have done so and after strolling through the communal passageway separating the two buildings and turning the handle, he found it locked.

Good old mum and dad, always predictable, mused a smiling John to himself looking around for another way to access his own back garden and home.

Moments later, he was shimming his way up the centrally located rain drain pipe that ran between each house's coal sheds, something he had done many times before if truth be known.

Then a moment of disappointment and dismay on finding that in his absence either his parents or next-door neighbours had built a burglar-proof glass roof panel blocking his exit altogether.

His path was blocked forcing him to descend back down to the ground annoyed and frustrated that proceedings had been halted; now he'd have to go around and across the back gardens instead.

Turning on his heels, John began a resigned walk back down the dingy passageway all the while looking and listening for signs of the helicopter but hearing nothing within earshot.

Luckily for him, he knew every single square inch of both his own back garden and all of the neighbouring ones as well, so getting there without being detected would not be a problem.

With that in mind, John left the relative safety of the covered passageway and began strolling out into the open air, rounding his dad's recently trimmed privet hedge and turning right.

With the searching helicopter presumably miles away, it would be a simple matter of cutting around and over the trio of back gardens on the other side of the row of council houses.

Choosing the neighbour's house two doors along because of its unfenced access and concrete slope, John knew that he could vault the low wooden fence into the rear garden area.

He did just that, finding himself standing in the familiar garden of the Butnal family looking to his right at a sight that never failed to impress and delight him.

An area the size of two football pitches had been divided into a dozen or so elongated rectangular gardens, his own being a short stone's throw away.

A moment later, he strode over to the waist-high fence and went to climb it, only to catch his leading foot and tumble headlong down onto the flower-lined border gasping for breath.

"Damn it," groaned the winded boy feeling slightly embarrassed by his own clumsiness and stupidity. He'd clambered over it lots of times before without falling so why now of all times?

It was whilst he lay pondering his bad footing that he heard the sound he'd been dreading, it was the returning helicopter and it was coming his way.

It galvanised the horizontal boy into action. John scrambled to his feet, only to realise that he had landed awkwardly in the fall and sprained his left wrist on impact with the ground.

That didn't matter, getting caught did, mused John as he ran as fast as he could across his next-door neighbour's garden; the soft grass beneath his feet allowed him to hear how close his possible captors were to him.

There was little doubt in his mind that the approaching rotor blades were only a couple of hundred feet away heading straight down Trinity Road towards him; he had scant seconds to find a place to hide.

Reaching his own garden fence, he once again got it wrong, the desperate boy clipping the very top and landing heavily amongst his dad's crop of potatoes, flattening several plants as he did so.

There was no time to count the cost of the fall both to him or the potato plants as the helicopter continued uninterruptedly as if homing in on him somehow or other.

Climbing back up onto his feet, John galloped through the rows of thigh-high potato plants and onto the paved pathway heading at speed for the family home back door.

His intended target and hiding place was the outside loo which was directly opposite the back door, all the while hoping that his parents had done the right thing and not let him down.

If they were so predictably methodical as he suspected them to have been, then they would have helped him no end; if not, then he'd be in very real trouble.

With the inbound helicopter almost on top of him, John took the nine garden steps five at a time in practiced fashion before racing the last few metres passed the red shed door to the house itself.

Suddenly, and to the boy's annoyance, the helicopter appeared in his peripheral vision over to the right-hand side just as he got to the back door area and ducked into the tiny alcove.

Had they seen me? mused a panting John turning left and pushing open the outside toilet door. All he could hope for was that the crew had not caught sight of him at all.

Closing the heavy wooden privy door behind him and ducking down as low as possible, he squatted and listened, noticing as he did that his parents had not let him down after all.

There, on a hook half way up the inside toilet door, was the key for the rear entrance. They must have somehow suspected that he would return home and left it there for him.

Removing the key from its hook, he utilised the outside toilet to relieve a particularly full bladder whilst listening as the helicopter circled for a while and then departed.

A quick look out through the tiny loo window revealed that the helicopter had indeed gone on its way leaving him to walk the short distance across the alcove to the back door and in.

That was exactly what he did, pulling open the loo door once he'd remembered to flush it, then stepping onto the back step, the key held out expectantly in his right hand.

Despite the fact that he was all alone apart from the searching helicopter, he still took a look around just in case before quickly returning to the matter at hand.

With a sense of relief and satisfaction, John gently inserted the key into the lock and turned, feeling it click comfortingly in his hand; it was a moment to savour.

Silently thanking his parents for leaving the key there for him, John turned the handle and pushed the door open, stepping quickly inside and closing it behind him.

The first thing he did was turn and lock the door, effectively sealing himself in a safe with the knowledge that he'd be sleeping in his own bed that night.

He had managed to elude all the technology available and reach his own home despite everything determined to halt him. Nothing could stop him from sleeping soundly tonight, he mused. Possibly a nuclear bomb…but nothing else.

31

Chapter Two

His first meal back home that night was cold baked bean and peanut butter sandwiches washed down with a couple of glasses of lemonade; a veritable feast as far as he was concerned.

Not only had his over-anxious parents left him his favourite food and drink, they had also thankfully kept the water on as well, cold only but it was a God send all the same.

A cold water wash wasn't very much fun but necessary, particularly as it was beginning to get dark outside leaving him with no gas or electricity available to use.

Two hours later, it was almost pitch black outside, made worse by the lack of any street lamps adding illumination. A sight that made John both apprehensive and excited.

No matter how intimidating the lack of street lights seemed to be to him Hornsea was still very much his town, he knew every shortcut and possible hiding place there was.

Luckily for him, his parents had not taken any of his things away with them, allowing him to better prepare himself for his forthcoming venture into an evacuated Hornsea.

Deliberately picking out dark trousers shirts and trainers, the excited boy began readying himself, dressing then digging out a pair of black gloves and putting them on.

In the next drawer down, he grabbed his penknife and ultra-thin pencil torch, then pocketed them; the candle flickering away as he did so.

Having decided not to bother with a hat of any kind, John made his way downstairs, ready to go out into the unprecedented darkness and have some fun.

Armed with the pencil torch and penknife, John stood at the back door with a sense of deep apprehension not really sure what to expect out there in the circumstances.

Was the helicopter flying around out over Hornsea as it had all day long? Surely he'd be able to see and hear it long before it reached him, no problem there he mused.

With confidence at an all-time high, he pulled open the door and stepped out into what was a darkness so intense that he very nearly went back inside again.

There was virtually no light anywhere to be found, making even his own garden completely black and potentially a minefield of possible accidents waiting to happen.

He had not come this far only to turn back and bottle it; it was now or never he told himself as he closed the door, leaving it deliberately unlocked in case he lost the key.

With a wildly pounding heart, John bit the bullet mentally trying to picture the familiar back garden in his mind's eye. Surely it wouldn't be a problem for him, would it?

He had no choice but to set off into the back garden and hope for the best taking several steps forwards, only to clatter into the plastic dustbin, nearly knocking it over as well.

An expletive later, he turned ninety degrees or so right and set off in a slow stagger into the unfamiliar blackness.

He soon reached the steps leading up to the higher part of the long garden. John tripped and fell headlong and face-first onto the elongated second concrete step.

Again he swore aloud having banged his right knee on impact. It hurt like hell as he lay sprawled out in grimacing agony still in his own back garden.

Following thirty seconds of painful knee rubbing, John found himself ready to continue, climbing to his feet and brushing the dirt and dampness from his clothing.

A quick feel around told him exactly where he was and in which direction he needed to go, setting off gingerly up the concrete steps, desperate to get used to the lack of lights.

Exiting home was ten times more difficult now that it was dark as once again he tripped and toppled onto several cabbages, ending up on his back between rows of his father's brassicas.

For the second time in as many minutes, John found himself flat on the ground; this occasion was equally embarrassing as the last, or it would have been had they happened in broad daylight.

Rising to his feet, the head-shaking boy stood gazing up into the night sky, not seeing anything at first then noticing a tiny pinprick of light, then another. The stars were coming out.

They bade well for him as far as casting a little more light on his surroundings was concerned, his eyes slowly adjusted to the surrounding darkness.

By walking along between the row of cabbages, John quickly made his way to the fence and climbed over, this time making it into next-door's garden without tripping and falling.

From there, it was a simple enough task to stroll across the garden lawn and over the next neighbour's fence; before long he was out onto the main road.

With his eyes fairly used to the conditions around him, John decided to turn right and stroll across the greenway, a triangle of grass with a row of local shops on one side.

Without the illumination from the street lamps, there was a weird eeriness that John didn't like as he reached the grass and began walking towards the unlit shops in daftness up ahead.

It was a walk he had made hundreds of times before in his twelve years living on the estate but never in such extreme darkness and lack of traffic; it scared him slightly.

There was still no sign or sound from the search helicopter at all, mused the ponderous boy on reaching the very centre of the greenway and stopping to peer all around him.

Hornsea was as silent as the proverbial grave as far as sounds and movements were concerned. His ears were humming like he had a sea shell up against them, eerily so.

A very slight breeze caressed him as he stood taking everything in. As he turned to gaze back at his own home, he thought he caught sight of something just beyond the houses across from it.

Was it the helicopter somewhere in the distance? Surely it could not be anything else. Then it sparked again, only this time even brighter than before.

No matter, he still had plenty of time to find somewhere to go and hide but for now, he was quite safe knowing the surroundings as well as he did.

One complete side of the greenway ran in a concave semi-circle with a road dissecting it midway, leaving three shops on each end, now locked and in complete darkness.

Setting off again, John strolled in the general direction of the shop on the far left, the family's local store and his own favourite newsagent.

He'd just reached the road between grass and shop steps when an enormous flash of light lit the sky over to his left. It had to be the helicopter but why couldn't he hear it?

A moment later, the light blinked off and all was dark again, making John wonder just what could have made it. Surely not a flash of lightning, not without thunder as well.

Then the entire section of houses including his own were lit up as if by a powerful beam of light but still no sound of helicopter rotor blades. Then he saw why.

He got the shock of his young life as an army land rover slowly came into view, one mounted with an extremely powerful spotlight amongst other devices aimed at noticing moving objects.

A shiver ran up his spine as he stared open-mouthed at this very real danger now facing him, one that would soon locate him if he stayed out in the open as he was right now.

With the land rover about to turn onto Trinity Road, its super trooperesque spot lamp illuminating everything it was aimed at, he could only peer around desperate for a place to hide in.

Then he remembered the nearby storm drain. Was it still there? Was it unlocked? It had to be, John told himself as he set off running as fast as he could hopefully to safety.

With the entire area around the greenway growing brighter with every passing second, the panic-stricken boy quickly reached the road that split the six shops his target moments away.

Knowing as he did that the storm drain was situated on the opposite kerb and opened outwards, John threw himself down sliding the last metre or so onto the strong metal grid.

Without bothering to look up, he grabbed the grill and yanked it upwards. To his relief, it came up and opened, clearly unlocked, the rusted grate squealing its protestations at his actions as it did so.

Night was about to turn to day as he began a rapid descent down into the cobwebbed depths, noticing en route that the super bright spotlight was now aimed at the row of shops and would pick him out like a sore thumb any second now.

With blind panic swamping his senses, he continued his hurried downward climb, all the while seeing the brilliant light slowly flit ever closer to him and the open storm drain.

Having descended low enough on the metal steps, he grabbed the cold metal cover and pulled on it, only to find it stubbornly stayed in place much to his grimacing annoyance.

All the frantic boy could think of to do was thrust both sets of fingers up and through the slatted grill then lean forward and allow his entire body weight to pull it down.

With the spotlight now perilously close almost upon him, John launched himself off the metal ladder altogether, the drain cover slammed down into place with an almighty clang.

The resulting closure left the dangling boy with only one way to go, downwards. John fell and landed painfully amongst the assorted debris and accumulated stagnant water several metres below.

John yelled out in unstoppable and unquenchable agony, only to bite his lip to silence himself, clambering to his feet and listening avidly as he peered up at the overhead grill.

It was light, occasionally extremely so as they searched for signs of life or movement. All John could do was climb the metal ladder and take a careful look outside.

He did just that, hauling himself up a rung at a time knowing as he did that the storm drain had a slightly raised sluice ramp allowing water to run in and him to peer out.

At first, he saw only darkness, nothing else. Had they driven on? Then he caught sight of a movement to his right, then an intense bright light hit him in the face.

He was temporarily blinded but his sight quickly returned in time for him to see the land rover turn from the main road onto the greenway itself heading straight for him.

Had they seen him? Surely not, or were they simply sticking to a pre-selected route through the town estate with variations so as not to appear static and predictable?

Then as he was staring at the approaching land rover, they fired the super trooper beam straight ahead hitting him so unexpectedly that he lost his grip and fell.

Again, he found himself clattering down on to what was a fairly soft water-logged ground, this time banging the back of his head on something solid on impact.

Despite what was going on outside, John could only lay in a sea of foul-smelling garbage, moaning softly, half-blinded, not caring if they found him or not.

After what seemed ages, the horizontal boy struggled to his feet hearing a high-pitched noise. He didn't like the sound. Was it a rat or more than the one?

Despite the feeling of nausea, he quickly reclimbed the metal ladder and took a cautious look out through the slatted grill; all was back to being almost pitch black. They had gone.

The estate around him was in eerie blackness again as he pushed up the cover of the storm drain and climbed back out, lowering it down into place as gently as possible.

A quick look around him revealed that he really was all alone, save for the seeming electrical disturbances that he now knew to be more vehicles patrolling the town as well.

It was not going to be as much fun as he originally anticipated, mused the frowning boy to himself as he weighed up the odds of managing to hide from the range rovers and helicopter.

Then again, perhaps if he stayed off the main roads altogether and kept to back doubles, he should have some fun after all. Yes, what he had to lose.

With that thought in mind, John took the side road that dissected the row of local shops finding disconcerting to walk along the centre of Beresford Avenue with no traffic anywhere in sight.

In fact, there were no parked cars anywhere, creating an unnatural silence that seemed to make him paranoid in the unlit blackness he knew so well in daylight but not so much now.

At the other end of Beresford Avenue, he reached a T junction with John going left down a small but steep hill, stopping at the foot where the main road intersected.

Whereas everything around him was very dark due to no streetlamps, he could still make out occasional bright flashes of light in several directions.

It was clear to him that at least three maybe four spotlight-mounted land rovers were deployed in and around the town; one was down at the seafront, where he was headed.

From what he could make out, at least two other vehicles were in the town centre, but it was the bright flashes coming from the direction of his own home that worried him most.

The searching vehicles were set at very close intervals between one another, which gave him less time than he'd have liked to move around in the tirath be known.

With that thought in mind, he sprinted diagonally across Trinity Road and darted as stealthily as possible past the ambulance station, then left ducking into and behind a set of garages.

Even in that darkness, he knew exactly where he was; the garages standing directly opposite the local scout hut and barely half a mile from the seafront itself.

He had evaded capture so far but for how much longer, mused the pensive boy peering upwards but there was no sign of the helicopter that had dogged his arrival earlier on that day.

With that thought in mind, John strolled to the far end of the garages via a narrow passageway, again stopping still and peering out into the silent blackness to get his bearings.

The town around him was lit by occasional pinpoints of bright lights allowing him to know the whereabouts of each car patrolling, thus giving him time to find a suitable hiding place.

That was the theory he told himself whilst gazing back in the direction of his own home, noting at once that the oncoming patrol was somewhere near the greenway. He still had plenty of time.

With a sudden and renewed conviction, the confident boy set off across recently cut wet grass heading for the road leading down to the nearby seafront.

As he strolled from the damp grass onto a fairly wide pavement, John began to realise that he would have to play cat and mouse with each patrol, a game he was born to play and win.

To his left, he knew ran a narrow lane called 'Bank Terrace', a tree and house-lined area normally off limits to most children due to its lack of street lighting.

It also had the reputation of being both haunted and home to the bogeyman, thus scaring most kids from going there after dark but not him.

He'd been down there and lived to tell the tale, instantly giving him a well-deserved reputation amongst his peers. Now he'd gladly sprint along the lane if a patrol came out of the blue.

Luckily for him, all was quiet as far as the patrol and the conspicuously absent helicopter were concerned, giving him growing inner belief and confidence with each passing second.

Again a brilliant beam of light swept upwards and across the unlit town he knew so well, this time from the very centre itself; then a second flash in a diagonal line somewhere up ahead.

With extreme caution, John continually peered around him in all directions as he strode along Burton Road, a half-mile stretch dog legging right to end at the sea wall itself.

Spotlight beams flashed around and above the evacuated town as if in wartime from the roaming land rovers constantly searching for any signs of criminals out looting the danger zone.

Still no sign of the annoying helicopter; had they decided to use it in daylight only? Yes, that had to be the reason. This was going to be easier than he thought it would be.

With the spot lamp-bearing land rover behind still back on the estate he lived on and the vehicle in front had left the area altogether, he decided to run the short distance to the seafront up ahead.

A couple of minutes later, he got there leaning on the concrete wall and looking outwards, hearing but not seeing the waves pounding ashore in the absolute blackness in front of him.

It was a strangely disturbing scenario as far as he was concerned. He stood unable to see the turbulent North Sea crashing onto the beach, its danger only too real should he have to climb over it to hide.

Dangerous or not it was a captivating sight, mesmerising the boy with its monotonously powerful restlessness; so much so that he failed to notice the vehicle approaching from behind.

Turning suddenly, he was shocked and surprised to see the land rover had already turned the corner and was driving towards him, its strong spot lamps pulsing outwards in all directions.

He had to find somewhere to hide but where? He did not fancy leaping over the sea wall one little bit but where else was there? Then he remembered something.

There might just be a way to avoid detection, only there may not be enough time to get there. 'There' is the large two-storey building overlooking the resort's boating lakes.

It was a good two hundred yard sprint to get to it with the light-spouting land rover already over halfway along the road. It would be touch and go but he had to make it.

Running as fast as he possibly could, John gritted his teeth and headed along the half-mile-long coast road hoping to make it to the boating lake house before the spotlights caught him.

All he could do was utilise his own knowledge of the resort to good effect and get the better of the people driving the land rover who only had a map to guide them.

With both lungs burning, he took a quick look back over his left shoulder, seeing straight away that the search vehicle had indeed reached the sea wall but was concentrating its beam on the south cliffs and caravan camp beyond.

His own turn-off place should be just a few more steps ahead on his left. Yes, he looked to have gauged it right in the darkness, diving for the gap just as a bright spear of light lit the entire length of the coast road itself.

Had he done it, groaned a grimacing John Philips to himself as he lay nursing an already damaged left wrist, but not for long as the light began growing brighter in intensity.

The land rover had already started along the coast road; he had to find a place to hide with pain etched on his young face. John got to his feet and ran up a set of worn concrete steps suddenly desperate to evade capture.

Forgetting the throbbing agony in his left wrist, he turned right, launching himself up a second flight of concrete steps realising as he did that they were bound to stop and take a look around.

Again he mounted a third set of eight concrete steps reaching the second upper level, the observation deck providing a superb view of the entire seafront and beyond.

Where had he managed to hide from his friends the last time he played and won a game of hide and seek? Then it came back to him just as the land rover stopped and its doors flew open.

The roof itself, yes, that's where he had gone but that was in broad daylight, now it was pitch black and he might fall and kill himself should he slip and lose his footing.

Now he was under pressure to make the climb as voices followed flashing torches from the halted Range Rover, not to mention the spot lamp beam already sweeping the area below him.

Gritting his teeth, John ran to the very end corner and climbed up onto the outer handrail itself, gripping the thin support beam to help retain a precariously dangerous balance.

With the spotlight slowly heading his way and torches coming up to the top level, he had to act fast. Using every ounce of energy, he reached up, grabbed hold of the upper beam and threw himself bodily upwards.

Like a high jumper doing the straddle manoeuvre, he felt for then found his feet connected with the roof itself, pushing his body and rolling onto the top of the building just in time.

All the panting boy could do was lie as still as he possibly could and hope that none of the people below had caught sight of him. So far so good, they had not.

John held his breath as several security men came to the edge and stood talking together, the powerful spotlight beam picking out places he recognised whilst a light breeze tousled his hair.

It had worked like a charm mused the horizontal boy listening as the searching security men returned to their vehicle and drove slowly away, leaving him smiling to himself in the icy darkness.

His smugness was short-lived as he noticed the land rover drive to the very end of the narrow coast road about to turn left; it would allow them a very clear view of the rooftop and him as well.

He now had the unenviable task of rapidly descending his hard-earned hiding place in order to avoid possible detection by those aboard the distant land rover.

With the wind rippling over his already freezing cold clothes and body, John began lowering himself down into the surrounding darkness all the time feeling for a decent foothold.

Using both arms to slow the rate of dropping, the grimacing boy felt his left foot come into contact with the wooden bannister at the same moment a bright beam of light struck him.

The sudden fear of discovery forced him to go for broke, letting go altogether and using self-preservation, he grabbed the upright pillar, and then dived forward into the darkness below.

John landed in a painful heap on the cold wooden upper floor of the resort's boating lake house, groaning in agony as light lit up his surroundings for a while then went off altogether.

Judging by the warm trickle on his forehead, he had cut himself in the fall, landing awkwardly and grazing both knees as well as he lay counting the cost of his tussle with lady luck.

Climbing slowly up to his feet, he leaned over the handrail and squinted out into the blackness, only to notice another spotlight arcing over the final few bungalows of Burton Road.

John knew instantly that it was the very next land rover along approaching the seafront; he was going to have to do it all over again if he wasn't careful.

Not particularly fancying another spell atop the boating lake house, he rounded the upper level, descended the three sets of concrete steps to the coast road and began running.

Despite knowing the resort as well as he did, it still felt odd with absolutely no light except an occasional showing of a semi-circular moon and several stars to help.

Keeping a constant look behind for the approaching land rover, John made it to the amusement and pleasure beach end of the coast road, noting that the search vehicle was still nowhere in sight.

With plenty of time on his hands, he made it a priority to stop and try each and every door he came across, especially the burger and hot dog stalls, but they were all locked.

"Damn it," groaned a disappointed John Philips as hunger pangs fluttered like frightened butterflies in his stomach…scrumping. Yes, that was it; he'd go scrumping.

If he recalled from last year's gang scrumping sessions, the best apple and pear orchard was owned by the local vicar but he lived in the very centre of town.

That area of Hornsea would be swarmed with security people and others so getting there would be dangerous if not impossible to some but not for him.

There were he knew ways and means when it came to getting from A to Z, especially in a small seaside resort like Hornsea, all he had to do was cut through the town's park and he'd be there.

A quick look south told him that the land rover was well on the way towards him, giving John just enough time to get clear of the area before it reached the pleasure beach itself.

He was still very much in danger of accidentally getting caught in the vehicle's powerful spotlight at any moment as he sprinted across a large piece of open land in the opposite direction.

Peering left as he went revealed that yet another spotlight bearing land rover was even now patrolling his council estate on its way around and through the town.

Once back undercover, he slowed to a more sedate stroll checking ahead on each turn just in case someone had been posted on corners, but he needn't have worried; all was quiet and still.

The nearer he got to the resort's Hall Garth Park, the more noise and activity he seemed to be hearing but how was that possible he thought to himself surely it was closed and empty.

Stopping at the town's congregational church, John peered around the corner having reached the main junction feeding left onto the high street and right down to the Hijge Public Park.

Something was going on in the park itself but what, mused the curious boy as lights flashed to his left presumably from one of the ubiquitous land rovers fitted with powerful spot lamps plus other image-finding devices setting off.

With another one not too far behind him, John knew that his time could not be wasted and with that in mind, he took a deep breath, and then ran across the road.

The tall spire of the congregational church was not visible at all nor was hardly anything else in the claustrophobic blackness blanketing the normally busy well-lit seaside resort.

There was light though it was emanating from the park itself, noises as well, talking and banging sounds, making him suddenly desperate to find out who was making them and why.

With his curiosity well and truly piqued, John made his way along passing a handful of local shops, then edged in between several massive plastic wheelie bins he knew always stood there.

Despite the intensely sickening smell of rotting food, the wide-eyed boy peered out around the edge of the end wheelie bin and thin straggly hedge that ran into them.

What he saw left him both breathless and fascinated as lots of white-coated men and women were seemingly busy constructing some kind of makeshift building of one kind or another.

The Hall Garth Park he knew was divided into two areas, the part before him was a semi-crater the size of a football pitch that tended to flood in wet weather.

It was a kiddie's play area with swings, a rocking horse, and a metal roundabout in one corner to the right of a long concrete slope that fed in from the wrought iron park gates.

The wooden cabin that lay at the foot of the entry slope was no longer there having presumably been removed to make way for the weird-looking building they were busy constructing.

From where he was hiding, he could just make out that the park's decorative gates had also been removed as well as the length of the hedge on either side of it.

That's strange, mused the frowning boy peering at the work being done over in the park gulley. "Were they anticipating the arrival of the atomic bomb here of all places?"

The north and west slopes rose fifty feet or so and levelled out to be a nine-hole golf course being four times the size of the lower portion John was gazing at but not for long.

A sudden flash of brilliant white light from behind caught him completely by surprise, forcing the shocked boy into action. John almost toppled over whilst shuffling out of sight.

Luckily for him, that particular land rover turned left, heading towards the town's marketplace, leaving him safely unobserved at least for the time being.

That close shave told him that it was time to leave the area immediately which he was quick to do, retracing his steps back up the incline past the tiny row of unlit shops.

Instead of going left back towards the seafront, he turned right and began a careful stroll into the park's upper area, making out absolutely nothing in the pitch blackness as he went.

All he could do was go on gut instinct and automatic pilot with no moon or stars to help him, only a faint glow from the work down at the lower park filtering up over the hilltops available.

Soon even that faint glinting of light was extinguished, leaving him with the unenviable task or going the full length of the undulating grassy park seemingly blindfolded, it was so dark.

Hopefully, there were no men posted in the park around him, all wearing infrared night-vision. Then again wouldn't that be an expensive waste of money in the circumstances?

The uninviting darkness he was inching his way through forced him to take out his trusty pencil torch, using its thin powerful beam in very short bursts from behind his cupped left hand.

The extra-curricular light, though useful, did not really help him as he felt the ground begin a downward incline, rolling him into a natural gulley he recognised as part of the golf course.

In his mind's eye, he knew exactly where he was in relation to his required destination: the vicar's orchard. He could almost taste those sweet apples, he was within sprinting distance.

He was still going to have to be careful, one wrong step in the unforgiving blackness might mean an unwanted accident and that he could ill afford to even think about.

There was a high dry stone wall running along the entire length of the park from the picturesque parish church around and behind the vicarage's rear garden and orchard.

The surrounding parkland filled his nostrils with the scent of wet leaves and somewhere in the blackness, an owl hooted his name, or so it sounded like to him anyway.

Remembering not to drift left and end up wandering into a patch of dangerously tangled bushes that could badly scratch him, John deliberately kept right avoiding the big trees en route.

By cleverly utilising the pencil torch thin and welcomed beam of light, John managed to avoid the bushes altogether, knowing that there was a way over the high wall just up ahead.

The extreme lack of any light at all made for very slow progress, even though he knew that the place he wanted was only another ten metres up ahead, he still needed to be careful.

Each time John used his pencil torch, he turned to face the high stone wall so. as to keep the beam of light out of sight should a land rover drive along the main road and notice it.

Suddenly, he was there and stood peering at the way up and over the eight-foot-high stone wall. It was a tree but no ordinary one as far as he was concerned.

This tree had a very thick gnarled trunk rising in an S shape before carrying on straight again to its full twenty feet or so in all besides the wall itself.

The weird kink in the tree trunk allowed knowledgeable locals to use it like a stepping stone to climb up and over the wall as a shortcut from the park to the town's nearby high street.

Putting his pencil torch to good use, he grabbed the trunk and climbed up onto the natural tree ledge, and from there, he scrambled his way onto the wall itself.

Without stopping to think, John stood atop the cement-topped stone wall and glanced all around him. It was only when he saw lights flashing very close by that he began climbing quickly down. After lowering himself down to the ground, he was pleased that he was still undiscovered and able to continue without worrying about having to remember any possible escape routes.

Having scrumped from the vicarage orchard many times before, he knew exactly where he was even in the pitch blackness around him; it was his home town after all.

He was standing on the grassy grounds of the local hall beside the St Nicholas parish church over to his right leaving the vicar's orchard to his left-hand side.

The only way he could possibly be seen was via a vehicle going by the open arched gateway and spotting him exactly where he was right now, he had to get going.

With that thought in mind, he turned and began walking towards the orchard itself, almost tumbling over as he forgot about the downward incline leading over to the trees themselves.

Instead of looking on the ground for landfall apples, John put plan B into operation, deciding to climb up the nearest tree and grab fresh ones at will.

It took quite an effort with no light available to assist him at all but after a couple of near mishaps, he ascended the tree and began seeking out the apples.

After finding and eating the first two or three, he began to get sick of apples and scrumping altogether, taking only one bite and then tossing the remainder away.

All the while he was climbing trees and chucking half-eaten apples around, the bright super troopers of light continuously flashed in the dark sky acting as a warning to him.

Eventually, he got tired of scrumping and decided to head home. The question was which was the best way to avoid possible detection from the annoyingly persistent land rovers?

Going back through the dangerously dark park was not a very good idea but there may well be another even safer choice, one that would keep him off the roads all the way home.

The route he was thinking of would take him through the grounds of his old primary school, the one he attended prior to his parents sending him to boarding school.

Once passed the primary school, he would nip up onto the now long disused and dismantled railway line, taking the single cinder track back to the estate the rest would be easy.

With one last apple thrown hard over the stone wall into the park, he left the orchard, making his way to the open archway. John peered out left and then right to find if it was all clear.

There were flashing lights to be seen but not close by telling the wantaway boy that his plans might just work, he'd have to sprint hard to avoid the oncoming land rover.

That was exactly what he did, setting off in a sprint along the unlit but still familiar pavement all the time staring ahead at the powerful beams of light coming ever nearer.

It was only a couple of hundred paces but it seemed an eternity to the desperate boy frantically racing against time to reach the next right-hand turn before they caught him in their sights.

Halfway there he suddenly realised that the fast approaching land rover had already reached the congregational church and began the sweeping turn just up ahead.

With searchlight beams flashing away ahead of weaker headlamps coming, it left him seconds from the turn and about to be caught like a fly in amber any moment now.

The powerful spotlight arced well ahead of the approaching land rover flashing and flitting along from shop to shop, reminding him that he dare not let them see him at all.

Wanting only to disappear from view altogether, John sprinted as hard as he could for the turn just up ahead, dashing across the unlit road just as the land rover came into view.

Fear and trepidation flashed through him as he continued down the dark cul de sac, knowing that the rear school gates were only a stone's throw away. Then disaster struck.

In the near blackness and in his all-consuming desire to avoid detection, he ran into something and fell forward, landing painfully on the concrete slabbed pavement.

Some idiot has gone and left their flaming pushbike lying on the ground, snarled the shocked boy to himself as he lay in agony in front of the town's fishing tackle shop.

He didn't have time to lay there feeling sorry for himself, not with the gadget-laden land rover about to appear any moment now; he had to get going.

Scrambling quickly back up onto his feet, he instantly felt his left kneecap spasm as pain swept through it, not helped by the realisation that his trousers had ripped open there as well.

"SHIT!" A grimacing John Philips exclaimed having noticed the brilliant spotlight beam sweep across the area where the main road reached the junction he was close to.

Turning on the excruciatingly painful knee, he began a waddling lope along the cul de sac leading he knew to the rear of the old primary school and his hopeful passage back home.

The damaged knee turned out to be only superficial and not as life-threatening as he had thought; John found himself able to run it off the further he went.

As luck would have it, the land rover did not turn left but went straight on, leaving the relieved boy to continue unhindered and able to better enjoy the journey.

The unnatural lack of any lights whatsoever made everything look different even to him. He grew up in and around the town, yet even he had to think hard about where he was walking.

On reaching the school gate, he found that climbing over it was not going to be quite as easy as he had anticipated; for one thing; it was completely downward slatted leaving no hand or footholds anywhere in sight.

The only way over would be to vault it, which he duly did. John used his good leg to launch himself bodily upwards to straddle it, hauling his bad leg up and over en route.

Unfortunately for him, he landed on his gammy leg finding himself falling to the floor again, groaning loudly but not caring who heard him in the surrounding darkness.

He knew exactly where he was at that moment in time, laying on the tarmac driveway close to the mixed infant's block, moaning and nursing a twisted left kneecap.

Two minutes later, he was back up on his feet limping awkwardly along the winding driveway he knew led to the quadrangle at the front of the much larger primary school itself.

Even though he knew the town as well as he did, there were still places that felt distinctly claustrophobic, even downright frightening, it was so very dark.

On the other side of the primary school ran what was known by locals as the viaduct passageway; it was a narrow shortcut linking the town centre with the Hornsea Burton Council Estate.

The viaduct passageway ran across the local stream dyke on its journey but more importantly to him, it also crossed the old ex-railway line that once linked Hornsea to the city of Hull.

John had to admit that because there were no street lamps on, it was not quite as much fun as he had originally hoped it would be. Nevertheless, it was still an adventure after all.

There were four possible exits from the school grounds—firstly the gates to his immediate left leading straight onto the high street; definitely not the one he wanted.

The other three were single wooden gates and each one fed out onto the viaduct passageway and that was where he was heading for in the surrounding darkness.

He was halfway across the quadrangle when the worst possible thing happened, the entire area around him was suddenly lit up as the next land rover along turned into the main entranceway.

All he could do was stand stock still and stare at the oncoming vehicle trapped like a fly in amber, his mind urgently searching for a place to hide but there was nowhere at all.

Then he remembered the old gravel bunker just behind him. It was there attached to the school wall to use when it was slipper but to his memory was never full of anything at all.

Turning and sprinting all in one motion got him to the gravel bunker a split second before the land rover rolled to a halt and its powerful spotlight began sweeping the quadrangle.

Unluckily for John, someone had broken with tradition and done the dirty to him in the process. Luckily, I was only half filling it and leaving hopefully just enough room to climb in and close the lid.

He did just that, desperately hoping that they had not seen him do so, lying uncomfortably in an awkward position that began to hurt his left knee quite a lot.

The seconds passed painfully along as he lay grimacing away in the damp-smelling gravel bunker; the chance of sudden discovery not helping his butterfly-filled stomach one little bit.

After what seemed ages, he pushed the heavy metal lid upwards to check on conditions out in the quadrangle. All was in extreme darkness once again; they had gone.

Pushing the heavy lid open to its fullest, John began climbing his way out of the uncomfortable confines, groaning as he did so, his left knee throbbing agonisingly as he straightened up.

"Ooh! Aargh…oh dogshit!" The pain-stricken boy spat rubbing at his damaged knee whilst attempting to walk, finding himself nearly falling over like a drunken man trying to act sober.

After staggering for fifty feet or so, he managed to keep on his feet heading past the huge quadrangle and along a narrow lane leading to the very far end of the primary school grounds.

It was a lot harder than he had thought it would be having to negotiate his way between buildings and trees in pitch blackness even though he knew his surroundings very well indeed.

Apart from occasionally wandering into and onto the flower beds, it was a long frightening walk, especially in almost pitch blackness with hardly any sound whatsoever from the nearby houses.

Then he remembered his pencil torch, surely no one would see a light where there are no roads at all, only school fields and fences all around; it was a brilliant idea.

It was the perfect thing to do in the circumstances, mused John as he fished it out and flicked it on, the torch's beam of light illuminating his way ahead very well indeed.

With excellent illumination to guide him, John soon made it to the opposite end of the primary school grounds, turning to shine his torch back in the direction he'd just come from.

He was now stood with the school canteen over to his left and a huge building called the 'Mascot house' immediately behind him; the latter being the town's nightclub and casino.

If memory served right, he only needed to press a certain area of the wooden fence to open up a three foot gap wide enough to slip through and he knew the exact place as well.

Or at least he thought he did. John spent the next few minutes tapping and pressing at a certain area of the fence, only to find it by accident leaning against the panel itself.

With a reddened face, he scrambled his way through the newly found gap, the torch still glaring away at the cloying darkness as he quickly replaced the irksome panel again.

The grounds of the 'Mascot house' were mercifully small and after twice walking into bushes, he reached the main gates and began to climb up and over as he had many times before.

Landing with practiced agility, John stood listening and looking in all directions, the torch snapping off in the process; his efforts were rewarded by tomb-like darkness with occasional flashes from one of the searching land rovers.

From what he could detect, one land rover was leaving the council estate whilst another had reached the beach area. He'd remain out of sight just so long as he kept his torch switched off.

With the main road a good quarter of a mile away in the distance and nothing moving on any of the side streets around him, he was quite confident of getting back home unseen.

Setting off, he rounded a wire metal bar-topped barrier put there to slow down speeding cyclists and strode down a short but steep footpath and along to the concrete viaduct bridge.

There was he knew a small muddy track on either side leading up onto what was once the railway line from Hornsea to the city of Hull, now a cinder track long overgrown but a well-known shortcut to those who lived there.

Once up on the cinder track, he turned right and began walking, keeping as best he could to the very centre whilst peering into the darkness on his far left to check on the land rovers.

With the beam-sweeping land rover having exited the council estate and now about to disappear behind a row of holiday cottages on its way to the coast, he risked his torch again.

Although the long cinder track was well-known to him, so was the eight foot wide stream dyke that ran across its path spanned by a wide planked bridge and a gas pipe close by.

Without the light from his torch, he may well end up missing the plank bridge altogether, ending up falling into the stream itself, which he did not want to have happen.

Then again, he couldn't afford to take too much time either what with the land rover patrols set at regular intervals and fitted with heat movement detection equipment as well as spotlights.

Slowing slightly John reached the stream dyke and strolled over the bridge remembering to keep the torch cupped just in case the light just happened to be seen and investigated.

On a sudden whim, he shone the torch at the nearby gas pipe. A flood of memories of the past crossed, reminding him of his recent past at that very place, some successful others not so.

The idea had been to clamber onto the pipe and by using the metal side flats, waddle slowly from one bank to the other until one adventurous boy walked straight along the top.

After that, they all followed suit, some walking others running, and then one boy slipped and fell into the murky waters, after that they resumed the old method to cross.

A sudden faint flash of light told him that the very next car was already in the council estate and that he had to get going. It was imperative that he remain invisible at all times.

Rising from the slight hollow, John started a reasonably brisk walk along the partially overgrown cinder track remembering to cup his hands over the torch each time he flicked it on.

Soon, he was out of sight from the main road sandwiched between a very high bushy, bramble-packed elongated mound once a slag heap and tail trees to his left.

John also knew that the cinder track had another gap in it a few hundred metres ahead where the main road ran beneath what was once a train bridge long since demolished.

His plan was to exit the track in a further hundred paces or so at a place known locally as the Bank Terrace, a natural hollow of a lane filled with enormous trees and a haunting atmosphere.

Normally, he'd have thought twice about it but now with no light whatsoever, the old fear was gone; plus it was only a couple of streets from home and he couldn't wait to get back there.

A couple of bursts from his torch told him that he had reached one of a number of long muddy slopes leading down to the tarmac lane below. They were all extremely steep and very dangerous in daylight, never mind pitch blackness.

John chose the middle one of the three and with one last burst of torchlight began slowly edging his way forward. His only hope was to remain on his feet and not fall over at all.

He need not have worried, though, for one moment he almost lost his footing, suddenly finding himself running hard but remaining on his feet despite stumbling over rocks and branches.

Thankfully, he came to a halt standing on the smooth tarmac back lane having safely managed his descent. A quick look and listen revealed that he was all alone.

Turning to his left, John began walking, coming to a fairly steep but mercifully short hill leading to a junction; the right led to the main road whereas the left took him to the greenway and home.

No sooner had he taken the left turn, than he was almost caught in the full-beamed spotlight as the next land rover along swept around the greenway as had all the others before it.

With lightning reflexes, he leapt backwards hopefully without having been seen by those in the search vehicle; an action that was to prove invaluable as the spotlight did not return.

Keeping a careful watch on events from his hidden vantage place, he was soon rewarded by the sight of the gadget-laden land rover disappearing around the corner to continue its journey.

It was once again pitch black all around with occasional bursts of bright light from the search vehicle. He knew that it was time to go home whilst the going was good.

Setting off in a slow jog, he quickly reached the unlit greenway hardly recognising it in its current state but knowing his own estate's topography by heart.

Without stopping, he turned right and continued a steady run in the direction he knew his house to be. John was feeling tired but relieved to have made it back home undetected.

A quick check told him that the next search vehicle was still approaching the estate and not yet in range; it gave him a chance to use his torch to pick out his route home.

With newfound agility and dexterity, he made it across the back gardens without incident and was soon pushing open, stepping inside, then relocking the back door.

The thrill of making it safely and stealthily back home quickly turned to disappointment as he remembered that both electricity and gas had been switched off, leaving him in the dark but this time indoors, and with no hot water at all.

Stripping off his wet clothes, he bit the bullet and washed it in cold water. Once that was done, he wrapped himself in a clean dry fluffy bath towel and sat down on the sofa.

It was well after midnight yet he wasn't the remotest bit tired, his mind constantly replaying the events of earlier that night; so much so, that he rolled over and tried to fall asleep.

Sleep constantly eluded him at every turn, forcing him to seek another method of gaining his objective, remembering what his mum and dad did that made them both go to bed.

Oh yes, the drinks cabinet, mused the smiling boy suddenly recalling the few times he watched his mum and dad have a drink or two making them tired then they'd go to bed.

Keeping the warm bath towel wrapped tightly around him, John rose from the comfort of the sofa, waddled his way to his parents' well-stocked drinks cabinet and pulled open the doors.

Whiskey, brandy, and vodka were all instantly ignored and for very obvious reason, choosing instead a bottle marked 'Dandy & Burdock' as he liked dandelion and burdock; it was his favourite.

Grabbing the bottle and a tumbler, he again utilised the pencil torch beam to make his way back over to the sofa, climbing into a nice cosy position, and then he unscrewed the top.

Pouring out a glassful and putting the bottle down on the carpet, he took several gulps and swallowed. Something was horribly wrong; instead of a cool drink, there was inner agony.

It had smelt and looked like dandelion and burdock, only to find himself in agony and wanting to be sick. *What was that stuff?* asked John between coughs and wheezes.

He quickly reached the conclusion that his mother had simply emptied and then reused the bottle, filling it with homemade wine. Whatever it was, it tasted horrible.

It was so horrible that he took another careful sip with the same results, burning and coughing loudly as he shuddered beneath the fluffy bath towel.

He suddenly began to feel tired and sleepy; so much so, that he took another drink, then another, several more in fact, quite liking the feeling sweeping over him if the truth be known.

Moments later, he fell fast asleep there on the sofa wrapped in the bath towel and in the arms of Baachus, he was also safe from discovery and feeling no pain.

Tomorrow would be another exciting day and one he'd remember for the rest of his life.

Chapter Three

"Have we actually located that thing yet? It's been days and cost a lot of money and secrecy," voiced a concerned Christopher Smithlington without removing his gaze from the view through the portacabin window; the freshwater lake both soothing and frustrating the fearless colonel.

"Not yet, Colonel, though we have come across Second World War German bombers en route; still we have worked out that it is not made of metal therefore not magnetic," responded a smiling Bobby Brentbean glancing up from the monitor for the briefest of moments before returning to the screen in front of him.

"Still we should locate the ship in the next twenty-four hours and be ready to haul it out of there. What do you reckon, Susie? You've been a bit quiet just lately."

"I'm reasonably excited alright, who could have thought that a bona fide crashed but fully intact UFO would end up here in the middle of nowhere of all places," vented Susan Bartholomew from behind thick black-rimmed glasses; her point of view instantly picking up on by the clever colonel. "Actually, it's quite the opposite. The Holderness triangle is on the UFO flightpath, only it's so desolate around here that they keep their lights switched off just in case."

"Ha ha…very droll I'm sure, but we are about to extract a genuine flying saucer from another world from the reed and pike-filled lake out there any time soon," trilled the twinkly-eyed female technician spelling out what they all already knew. A slight breeze jangled the yacht mast ropes into a rhythmic clattering like wind chimes outside as she continued. "And I still can't quite believe how easily the locals ate up that atomic bomb story of ours, yet they did hook, line and sinker now wonders never cease."

"You are so right, Susie. Once our boys and girls saw that UFO fired on then splash down here in Hornsea Mere, we knew we had an unbelievable opportunity at long last," boomed a more than delighted Colonel Smithlington turning to face the woman in question, only to be interrupted by a loud beeping sound from Susan's own computer terminal. Suddenly, all eyes swept across her as she checked her computer screen.

"Colonel, they have located the vessel and are about to latch on to it and drag it over to us."

Her words were met with loud cheers from the entire room as the full implications of their amazing recovery suddenly sank in. It would be the envy of the entire world.

"This is it, people, we are about to make history. Let's seize the opportunity for ourselves before the outside world finds out and takes it from us."

"What do we do should ET turn nasty on us, Colonel?" A still smiling Susan asked, her question halting several of her colleagues beaming congratulations straight away such was the seriousness and possible danger they may well be facing.

"All I can offer is that whilst we might be about to open quite a colossal pandora's box that could have tragic consequences to all of humanity on one side of the equation," proffered her unsmiling superior officer and team leader as the room around him went strangely silent, all eyes and ears glued on the man responsible there on site.

"But on the other hand, it could offer a whole brand new and unmissable beginning for mankind in all directions. I personally think it's worth the risk, don't any of you?"

There was a mixed reception from those listening on, several shaking heads but mostly nods of agreeance and a visible sense of optimism that they were doing the right thing.

"Right then, now we've got it. We can wind down and take what I have been reliably informed from my grandchild as a chill pill. Well done, people," volunteered the confident colonel in response to the satisfying news that the unidentified flying object had been found but that it still had to be dragged or carried across the lake bed.

"It'll be getting dark soon so go and get some sleep because I reckon it will take a good few hours before they manage to get it to us. Good work and see you later."

They were about to witness history in the making and one massive leap for mankind all in one once the alien space ship was brought up and out of the depths of Hornsea fresh water lake.

Then they would see…

To John Philips, the extreme lack of light was an adventurous challenge; one he had again risen to as he lay on his belly peering across the Mere at the scene played out in front of him.

With monumental trepidation, he had successfully dodged several search land rovers to reach Hull road field heading for what he knew to be the perfect place to see the dredged out a bomb.

The field was usually full of cows but they had been evacuated. It still left a minefield of cow pats, which by use of brief bursts of torchlight, he managed to easily avoid.

Whilst managing to avoid stepping into cow pats, he completely forgot that the field itself dropped suddenly for seven or eight feet to a lower area level with the lake beyond.

Suddenly, the confident boy felt his lead foot slip away from under him and fell over backwards, hitting the ground hard and sliding several feet through thick wet grass.

The only thing going through his mind was that he hadn't been aided by one of the ubiquitous cow pats en route as he lay cursing his bad luck and forgetfulness.

Once back up onto his feet, he continued walking the relatively short distance to the nearby lake and his destination just up ahead.

Whilst it was noticeably lighter, thanks to what was going on across the water at the busy yachting area, he still had to be careful all the same.

Following a second fall after stumbling into a patch of tail thistles, he reached his chosen destination, a place he knew was an ideal place to view the peninsula and remain unseen.

Slowly but surely, he edged his way onto the place in question, a weeping willow tree whose thick trunk ran outwards horizontally over and partially into the murky freshwater lake itself.

Only the top half of the tree trunk was visible; the lower part was submerged as it stretched out some fifteen feet then changed direction and rose vertically upwards.

It would afford him the perfect place to view across the Mere hidden behind dense overhanging branches and thickly bowing leaves in total darkness.

The Mere-side peninsula was lit up like a Christmas tree as he edged his way onto the slippery-looking horizontal tree trunk lit in bursts by the torchlight beneath his cupped palms.

With the carelessness of a confident child, John dropped first onto his knees then allowed himself to flop down on his front to lay just inches away from the water slapping the green bark on either side of him.

Once he was comfortable, he reached into his coat pocket and eased out the pair of mini binoculars he'd remembered to put there for just such an occasion as this.

He didn't need them at first, everything was well-lit but nothing was happening; everyone wore white boilersuits, boots, and safety helmets as they strolled around exchanging notes.

A gigantic crane had been parked close to the water's edge beside a wide-decked boat, presumably to fish out the sunken atomic bomb when and if they ever came across it.

John lay there peering over the restless waters, hearing wavelets sloshing into the tree trunk on three of the four sides as people went about their business. Then all hell broke loose…

A high-pitched siren began sounding followed by men and women sprinting from nearly all of the collection of single-storey pre-fabricated buildings in all directions.

As the quizzical boy squinted towards the frantic goings on at the Mere-side area, the stretch of water immediately left of the headland began to glow.

A moment later, the colossal crane started up, the controller swinging its huge arm out and directly over the patch of glowing water, readying it to begin winching.

There was absolutely no doubt that they had found the bomb alright, mused the thoughtful boy as he peered across the lake at an awesomely eerie sight.

Instead of Merely glowing white, the waters began strobing in a myriad of colours, some he had never seen before as he put the mini binoculars up to his eyes and stared through them.

At first, he thought that the bomb was about to go off as the multi-coloured strobing grew brighter and quickened like a pulse, only to suddenly stop the moment it reached the surface.

Then he spotted two men on the wide-decked boat wearing scuba diving equipment, both waving directions to the man operating the crane lifting apparatus.

Once it was low enough, they attached what looked to be the end of a very strong length of web netting to it via two metal hooks securing it in place.

As he looked on, they each picked up the opposite ends and dived into the water, presumably heading for the other side of the bomb to lift it out of the lake itself.

The horizontal boy stared on as the two divers reappeared on the surface of the choppy freshwater lake and climbed out onto the waiting boat, both giving the thumbs-up sign.

With the signal sent, they fastened a second pair of metal hooks onto the crane hoist, then gave another thumbs-up, this time to the man operating the winch high overhead.

With a fascinated John Philips looking on, the crane driver began operating it, hoisting the still-submerged device up from the bed of the freshwater lake.

The water there sparked and fizzled around the strange-looking object as it slowly broke the surface and came to a halt some ten feet above the water.

Even to John, it was no nuclear bomb; for one thing, it was much bigger than any pictures he had seen, plus it was circular, saucer-shaped as it hung suspended in mid-air.

Whatever it was, it suddenly stopped sparking and slowly started to dull down as if someone or something had switched it off, soon it hung dark and foreboding only to be flooded with bright lights.

A split second before that happened, John noticed a pale green light blink on to one side of the unlit object directly facing him, then it shot across the water straight at him.

John blinked awake from the depths of a weird technicolour hazy dream, his mind ablaze with uncontrollable thoughts and emotions, his body tingling all over. Then he heard it…

"You are John Philips! We are John Philips! John Philips, we must flee this place to somewhere safe!" A strange-sounding voice in the very centre of his head informed, not the one he usually heard whenever he talked to himself but a completely different one altogether.

"Did you hear me, John Philips? They will soon work out what I have done and come looking for us. Come, you know the terrain."

"I…I…I er, I don't understand. Tha…that's not an atom bomb, it's…it's a space ship, isn't it? But who? How?" The suddenly disorientated, wide-eyed boy blurted, sitting bolt upright on the horizontal willow trunk, wondering what exactly had just taken place.

That booming voice? Where? How? mused a shell-shocked John Philips to himself, slowly rising to his feet only for the vibrating baritone to make him start.

"John Philips, I must insist that we immediately vacate from this vicinity if. we do not desire to be discovered and caught, it may already be too late."

"You…you came from that thing, didn't you? Wh…why?" The mind-blown boy gushed, finding himself wanting to ask a zillion and one questions to the mysterious booming voice, only to catch sight of flashing lights from the corner of his eye.

"Let us go right now, John Philips, please," begged the deeply booming voice as the boy turned to see that all hell had once again broken out across the water; the space ship was now lit up like a Christmas tree.

"We need to move from here, John Philips; there's no telling what they will do to us if we are found. We should go now and I will tell you all you want to know, yes?"

"I…er, I can't say that I understand at all but I agree that we should go away from here as fast as possible," agreed the suddenly wanted away boy taking a couple of steps along the half-submerged tree trunk, only to find himself lit up in a powerful beam of light as it swept slowly past.

"They have seen us, John Philips, it might already be too late, we must get to a safe place NOW!"

With those words sending alarm bells ringing away in his head, John began running as fast as he could not bothering to turn to face whoever had sent the search light beam across the water.

With speed the important matter in hand, footing was the very last thing on his mind, not caring what he trod on just so long as he reached the road in one piece.

"Faster, John Philips, faster. They will have already despatched some of your Earth vehicles to catch us," barked the stentorian voice, making him grimace with annoyance as he lost his footing for a third time, this time managing to stay on his feet thanks to the beam from his pencil torch.

"I…I'm doing my best here, it's not easy in these conditions," panted the breathless boy on reaching the upper level of the dark field, running blindly onwards towards the long wooden fence he knew ran across his path just up ahead.

"Utilise your light rod a little more, John Philips, but try not to let it become a beacon for others to follow," encouraged his irritating companion from deep inside his brain as John reached and ran straight into the slatted wooden fence before cursing loudly whilst jumping up and climbing over it.

Thankfully, the road was still in complete darkness with no cars or traffic at all anywhere to be seen, distant bright flashes of light indicated that some if not all search vehicles had been sent to get them.

Instead of turning left and heading for home, the knowledgeable boy went the other way, having already chosen another route and set off running in the opposite direction.

"Hurry, John Philips, hurry. We must not be caught; take flight, my bi-pedal friend," instructed the strangely calming voice urging him onwards, not that the energetic boy needed to be told as he continued along the unlit road now devoid of any parked cars whatsoever.

"We…we should be alright once we make it to the allotments up ahead, that's if they don't call for a helicopter," panted John whilst simultaneously staring into the darkness trying to pinpoint the actual entrance to the allotments and peering behind to see exactly where the pursuing vehicles were.

"Ah yes, 'Allotments', a place humans use to grow food in, but I suggest that you save valuable breath and Merely think what you want to say and we will be as one in our thinking," rattled off the voice inside his head, only for a noise he knew to send a chill of fear through him as the sound of distant helicopter rotor blades forced him to quicken his pace.

"Damn it, they've sent the daytime helicopter out for us as well. We've got to get under cover as soon as we can," blurted the super stressed boy sprinting like a gazelle along the dark footpath having noticed that at least one of the searching land rovers had turned onto the road and was speeding after them.

"It…it should be about here, ah yes, there are two grass tracks, one at either side. The first is the one I want; yes, there it is." On saying this, he launched himself left and off the smooth pavement on to a soft grassy uneven surface, instantly smelling a mixture of rotting leaves and compost as he did so.

"If they did not catch sight of you back there, they will begin searching the area in immediate proximity to our last known sighting then spiral outwards from there," ventured the deep rumbling voice lodged in his head whilst he struggled to keep his footing and direction, stumbling off the two foot wide pathway again and again in the darkness.

"If not, then they will soon be upon us, so move like the wind that encircles this planet of yours, John Philips."

"There are a bunch of garden sheds up ahead, they are all interconnected for local community purposes. Once we get inside, we can use it to get into the coal yard," grunted the breathless boy, again stumbling and almost falling, only to stay upright and carry on running, seeing hardly anything in front of him as automatic pilot kicked in.

"Once there, it's only a short distance to my parents' house and we will be safe there. First, we have to reach the sheds."

Knowing the town as he did, John was familiar with his present surroundings enough to put his faith in his own sense of direction and knowledge when it came to the crunch.

"I believe that we are about to be visited by the flying vessel you call a helicopter. Hurry, John Philips, we need to get undercover or they will see us any moment now," enthused his knowledgeable co-pilot with urgency in its tone of voice, not that he needed any more incentive himself as he took an impulsive intuitive guess and darted left.

It was unfortunately yet fortunately a big mistake with John running head first into a stack of corrugated iron sheets someone had placed there a few feet away from the shed door.

"OW! What the…damn it! This…this isn't happening. I…I've got to get out of here!" A panic-stricken John Philips shrieked from beneath the heap of rusty foul-smelling corrugated iron, only for the voice in his head to disagree, arguing against him doing so.

"John Philips, stop, do not move but lay perfectly still, remain hidden below these metallic objects. They are now immediately overhead and looking for movement on the ground."

With begrudging reluctance, he did as the voice requested even though he was in pain and discomfort from the jagged sheets as well as his injuries from the previous night's nocturnal escapades. "Lay as still as possible or our movements may give rise to suspicions. Our physical wounds are not serious so relax and I will ascertain our optimum moment to proceed."

"H…how will you kn…know?" The curious boy spluttered only too pleased to obey the slightly aggressive voice as if not liking to be interrupted whilst doing something else, multitasking perhaps.

What was the strange voice in his head? Where did it come from? Surely not from that gleaming metal disc, they pulled out of the Mere? But if not, from where then?

"All of your questions will be answered in the fullness of time, John Philips, but not here and now. You might want to know that your own senses have been boosted massively by me," droned the informative voice inside his head explaining what he could do in order to pinpoint exactly where the helicopter was in the unlit skies above.

"By utilising my own particular abilities within your primitive human brain, I can magnify the sounds reaching your ears and then reinterpret the readings thus."

"Oh, erm, I think I understand," bleated the badly scuffed boy, his baffled expression revealing the true extent of his knowledge on the subject, something not picked up on by the concentrating entity.

The boy was human after all and quite young, possibly shocked and slightly traumatised by earlier on when the out-of-body mind transfer took place, mused the off-world visitor.

"It has gone out of range, thus allowing us an opportunity to move on. Let us go right now, John Philips."

"Yes, yes, the sheds. We'll cut through them and on into the coal yard. Hopefully, they are still searching the fields and bushes back there," John ventured in response to hearing that the helicopter was now elsewhere and that they should go on, heaving the sheets of ribbed metal and crawling out from under them.

"I am assuming that they do not have any idea as to who you are at all, John Philips, or where you domicile, am I correct?" His deep-voiced entity quizzed as his host human stood on his feet peering around him in the near blackness getting his bearings, the helicopter close but nowhere in sight.

"Er no, or I hope they don't. Ah, there's the door to the shed," John informed it whilst striding to the row of sheds he knew were shaped like an army Nissen hut with a row of corrugated iron-topped shacks standing side by side and all interlinked.

Pulling open the outer door, he sauntered inside knowing about the sheds thanks to his dad's best friend owning one of the strips of allotments and bringing him to it from time to time.

Every allotment owner knew and trusted one another enough to make it a communal operation, sharing not only tools but food as well as the shed's layout suggested.

By use of his hand-shielded pencil torch, they were soon at the far end of the sheds then outside again. Even in the surrounding darkness, John knew exactly where he was.

A narrow pathway ran back to the allotments whereas a thigh-high brick wall fed onto the grounds of the town's long-defunct power station currently awaiting demolition.

It wasn't until he was over the wall and half way to the massive power station building that the sound of helicopter rotor blades filled the black night air overhead.

"They are about to discover us. Quickly, John Philips, we must escape their gaze," barked a clearly jumpy, nervous-sounding alien coinhabiting his mind, the boy had already jumped to that conclusion himself as he broke into a strong sprint towards the building up ahead.

"I...I can't see where I'm going. It's normally kept clear but I haven't been in there for quite a while so I'll have to be lucky and hope nothing happens," explained the fleet-footed boy on reaching and running straight on into the yawning archway without slowing at all, his only thought was in not getting injured in the dark interior.

"We are out of range of the equipment they are utilising to try and capture our movements but we must vacate this area as fleetly as possible," volunteered the still agitated voice continuing to urge him on to flee their desperate pursuers, freedom being the same commodity off Earth as well as on.

It was a heart-stopping journey as John ran from one end of the dilapidated power station to the other aided by his alien visitor as best it could in the circumstances.

"Move slightly left, John Philips, there seems to be an obstruction to the right, now straight onwards the path underfoot is clear."

With enormous relief, the tormented twosome arrived at the other end exit of the power station, the huge doors having been removed leaving it wide open for local kids and the elements.

"Whilst we may have eluded the helicopter, we are still at the mercy of the vehicles travelling via the road system arriving as we speak."

"Damn it, I know, I'll make a straight dash for home; we might just make it without being seen at all," John retorted whilst setting off at a brisk pace for the distant coal yard exit, spurred on by the equally desperate alien entity as lights began flashing ever closer to the fleeing boy.

On reaching the exit, one kept perpetually open by the owners to promote honesty and trust between locals and themselves, John stood panting in the gateway.

"What are you waiting for, John Philips? We have to keep running and escape capture," urged the voice in the centre of his head, sounding decidedly ill at ease at the thought of the boy's capture and what they would do to him once that was done.

"They are too close, they'd catch us in no time. I'm going to try something. I know this place better than them. I'll let them catch sight of me then out think them. Here goes."

"Yes, yes, John Philips, up the hill of nutty slack. You slipped and fell the last time you tried it remember?" The knowledgeable voice rattled off with unnerving familiarity as he stood in the open gateway awaiting the exact moment to step out into view to announce his presence but only momentarily.

"H…how did you know that I fell the last time I attempted the climb; you can't possibly know that," quizzed the furrow-browed boy in reply to the surprise statement made by the voice a moment earlier. Surely it could not have seen him back then so how…

"The same way that I know that your mother has brown eyes and your father wears a toupee, but now is not the time. We have got to get going right now, John Philips," blurted the panic-stricken entity as the searchlights flashed ever closer to them and the helicopter was not too far away either, there was no time to lose.

With gritted teeth, John took a step out, finding himself in full view of the land rover speeding towards him from the Mere-side, then turned on his heels and ran back into the coal yard.

"They have seen us, John Philips. Now get us away from here before they have time to signal our position to the helicopter."

John wasn't even listening as he was already heading for the second of the four deep brick-lined bunkers, three of which held coal whilst his one was filled with nuggets of nutty slack.

Without hesitating, he launched himself onto the mountain of hard nuggets, feeling them move dangerously underfoot but not slip down the higher he went.

"Faster, John Philips, faster, they are almost upon us," urged the agitated voice as a spotlight beam arced its way up the first bunker almost ruining his concentration in the process. The boy leapt for the top just as the land rover reached the coal yard entrance.

"Now, John Philips, use the strength of a Szydoozion guard to haul us up and over the top. Let us escape this nightmare. Pull, John Philips, PULL!" He did just that, utilising a power he never knew he possessed to heave and roll himself up and over the upper rim, and lay still as the land rover screeched to a halt down below.

It wasn't dark there for very long as the entire area in and around the coal yard was suddenly flooded with bright lights; it was time he wasn't there.

As he began rising from the deeply rutted ex-railway track, he caught sight of another land rover approaching at speed from the direction he intended heading and ducked back down again.

"John Philips, we need to move away from this place or we will be easily spotted by the helicopter. Come on, force yourself, we have got to go. Move, John Philips, MOVE!"

On hands and knees, he began a scurrying crawl across the uneven tracks with all hell breaking out behind him in the coal yard, the sound of distant rotor blades forcing him on.

"Move, John Philips, keep going; they must not see us," boomed the alien lodged deep in his brain, telling him what the young boy already knew as he reached the far side and literally crawled down the steep muddy slope sliding on his belly.

John lay as still as he could beside the wooden slatted fence listening avidly to what was going on around them as was his equally restless visitor, who finally broke the silence.

"Well done, John Philips, it appears that they have not located us yet. Make haste and we may yet escape their clutches."

It sounded good to him as he slid between the second of three horizontal slats that made up the wooden fence then stood up and took a dozen steps to his left-hand side.

There was he knew a solid high brick wall separating him from those anxious to lay their hands on both him and the off-world entity currently lodged inside his brain.

"What are you waiting for, John Philips? Surely it would be in our vested interests to leave this area whilst we can," quizzed the voice, sounding desperate to flee the area as quickly as possible, only for John to peer cautiously around the corner to see for himself what was going on.

As he watched, two more land rovers shot up the main road then turned noisily into the already crowded coal yard and once in, he grasped the opportunity with both hands.

With heart beating wildly, he turned and sprinted hard across the road knowing as he did that he was well out of range of the helicopter still hovering over the power station building.

"We have so far eluded capture but we must find somewhere that affords us time to rest and recuperate. You spoke of your family domicile, did you not, John Philips?"

"Yes, I did, and once we are there, we'll be perfectly safe. It's not too far away now," replied the breathless boy. John turned to check that there was no one anywhere in sight behind them before slowing to a walk at the next right-hand turn knowing they were reasonably safe.

"Where is it, John Philips? We must get undercover before they begin widening the search," droned the still slightly agitated voice as if somehow expecting to be caught any moment, even though John knew that the search for them was a wild goose chase which he had won.

"Relax, will you, it's quite literally just around the next corner, then they will never find us you'll see."

Five minutes later, he was cutting across the back gardens and home again, locking himself inside to an audible sigh of relief, one shared by the strange voice in his head as well.

Both were only too pleased to have evaded their would-be captors and made it to safety, but on the other hand, they were not dealing with amateurs but experienced professional people.

But for now, they were safe but for how long…

"Did you say that you actually saw the ET? What the hell did it look like?" A quizzical Brigadier Johnathon Harnabby growled having only just climbed into bed for a well-deserved early night to find himself disturbed by the scrambled hot line and its startling news. "Oh, and how in blue blazes did it manage to get out in the first place?"

"According to the report that I read, it was humanoid in shape, rather like a small child, two arms, two legs, a head, possibly green skinned we think," responded an unphased Christopher Smithlington, his thoughts only on the twinkling metal disc being winched onto the flat-backed vehicle whilst they spoke and nothing else.

"As to how it managed to exit its vessel, we don't actually know. There was a flash of light prior to the entity being seen but we are checking all external monitors as we speak."

"So they are humanoid after all; that's very interesting. The creature must have particle beamed itself out and across the waters. We must find it. Any ideas, Colonel?" The thoughtful brigadier on the other end of the telephone line mooted, not knowing the seaside resort at all but neither did the ET making catching it that much more difficult.

"Nothing concrete but we are scouring the area it was last seen with everything we have at our disposal," informed the positive-sounding colonel gazing with rapt awe as the off-world spaceship hung suspended on its hoist, a prize that more than made up for his losing the ET.

"In the meantime, we still have an almost intact flying saucer here at our convenience and if it wants its ship back, it will just have to come and get it."

"In that case, I'm ordering more men into the area to help find that blasted thing. We can't afford to have it escape from there and get into the press," snarled the officious brigadier stifling a yawn in the process, his manner veering towards the discourtesy often shown to lower ranks as is generally the way.

"Just make sure that you keep me posted on events, Smithlington, and remember we need that alien pilot dead or alive, got that? Now goodnight."

"Yes, goodnight, Brigadier. Though some of us will have to go without our precious beauty sleep and I guess it won't be you or any of your staff," replied the uncaring general, his gaze glued to the newly acquired identified flying object there in front of him out on the lorry. Its pilot's current whereabouts was another matter entirely. "I wonder what it's doing right now, and where?"

"I…I think that you are going to want to see this, General," trilled a furrow-browed Harry Petlingsea, fourth of five seated white-coated technicians working in the claustrophobic portacabin overlooking Hornsea's massive freshwater lake.

"What is it, Mister Petlingsea? We're rather tied up with the alien vessel at this moment in time. We are on quite a tight race against time here you know?"

"It's about the escaped alien. It seems that we were not the only ones in the area last night; it might be important."

His statement sent a ripple of curiosity through the mind of the inattentive general as several things leapt to the fore forcing him to leave what he was doing.

"I'll be right over."

Two minutes later, the duo were sat poring over a pre-recorded series of images, all night-time sequences taken during the alien's escape from its spaceship.

"What exactly am I supposed to be looking at here?"

"Look closely at the screen and I'll show you something that we have overlooked big time. Now see that scene there, it was taken at the moment the ET exited its flying saucer."

They both looked on as a brilliant pinpoint of light shot from the gleaming vessel and reached a horizontally sprawling willow tree where a humanesque figure got up and fled the scene.

"We know how he did it, Petlingsea, transporting himself across to dry land from its ship, I've watched that footage hundreds of times and its always the same. You're out of here right now!" An angry red-faced General Smithlington exclaimed through a sneer of undisguised disappointment, aiming a thin digit at the seated scientist staring back up at him.

"It is how the alien escaped, General, but it is not what I was talking about, this is; watch carefully."

On saying that, he tapped a certain key on the console and the scene on the screen slowly began running backwards, preceding the flash from the still dripping saucer to a sight that made the general's mouth loll open and stay that way.

A clearly astonished General Smithlington stared with wide-eyed amazement as the same horizontal willow tree appeared, only this time the human figure was there before the alien exit.

"Oh, sweet Jesus, th…there was someone out there watching us all that time. B…but who?" The utterly bemused general blurted gazing down at the figure on the tree trunk spying on events going on at the Mere-side and the spaceship in particular.

"Bu…but that's where the alien ended up! Oh my God! You don't think? W…we have got to identify whoever that person is. He's got our fucking alien!"

"If we can get a clear enough image of the face, then hopefully the mainframe computer could identify it and give us a name and address," ventured the knowledgeable technician in response to his panic-stricken superior's stunned reaction to what had taken place the night before.

"Right, listen up, people, we've got big problems here and I'm reassigning all of you to sort it out. According to our video surveillance cameras, we had two visitors last night," explained a much calmer, more relaxed, General Smithlington having switched to his normal professional mode and wanting to get the team working on the new task at hand.

"I want every one of you to concentrate on getting a half-decent view of our intruder's face so that we can identify and then capture the person currently housing the alien escapee. Let's get to work."

"What about the alien vessel? Shouldn't one of us continue on it?" Alicia Benprice from the very end computer console volunteered, aiming a trim digit in the direction of the tarpaulin-covered alien spaceship strapped to the back of a lorry outside.

"Forget that for the time being, I want everyone here working on the image out on that willow tree. We need to discover who it is and where to find both him and our alien visitor," barked back the frowning team leader. General Smithlington was not in the mood for anything other than finding the person who had defied the warnings and made it into Hornsea despite the security measures put in place.

"I'll grant a fortnight's leave to the first person to show me a clear image of the intruder; now get to work and find me what I am looking for."

On saying that, Harry Petlingsea despatched the series of video images across to the other computer consoles in turn plus all other of the pre-recorded items taken the night before.

Once that was done, work started in earnest spurred on by the proffered reward, the seated technicians suddenly desperate to try and identify the mysterious intruder as quickly as possible.

If ET thinks he can outsmart me and my team, then it can think again, mused the confident general as all eyes concentrated on the screens in front of them.

"Hiding in a human being was a pretty neat trick but it would not be long before the cat was out of the bag," growled the man in sole charge of 'Operation Retrieval'.

He'd personally see to it that whoever it was spying on them in a closed-down military-defended zone got locked away and the key thrown into the icy North Sea.

Then again, they did still possess the alien's saucer-shaped spaceship; presumably without it, the creature could not escape back into outer space.

Without it, the alien would be trapped here on Earth, so when it did return to the saucer, it would be captured and the secrets of travelling to the stars his for the taking.

"Your species is incredibly unpredictable and sometimes very stupid, John Philips. Humanity is only part way through its quest to find itself and its place in the multiverse," reeled off the overfriendly informative voice in the centre of his brain, having thankfully moved from his frontal lobe now that the danger of being caught was over.

"Rocket ships into space and moon landings when your people are hungry and dying of starvation on your world is a contradiction that should be addressed, am I correct?"

"You sound like my mum and dad, they are always going on about that kind of thing, they never stop," responded the young boy through a mouthful of peanut butter and Bovril sandwich, something that would be his staple diet if he had his way, which of course he didn't.

"Mum is always going on about the government spending taxpayers' money on the things it shouldn't and nothing on feeding and housing the homeless here and all around the world."

"Your mother sounds like a sensible person to me, but tell me, John Philips, why do the governments of your world do those things your female parent revealed to you?" The vexed voice probed as he continued chomping on the sandwich. It was as if the alien entity actually agreed with his clever mum, so perhaps she really was clever after all.

"According to dad, it has got something to do with PI, not the old fashioned mathematical one but a new thing about making money, now it's 'profit and interest'," explained a thoughtful John trying to recall his father's words as spoken by him to his mother as he tucked into dinner one time; not that he understood it all but he had quite a good memory. "My dad said that if big money-making companies around the world couldn't make any profit on something, then they wouldn't be interested in it, at least that was what I think he meant."

"PI equals profit and interest, now that is fascinating. You must tell me some more of this world of yours, like who is in charge of planet Earth?" The sometimes deeply annoying voice lodged inside his brain coaxed, again asking a question that for him was difficult to answer relying instead on things he'd picked up from his parents.

"Let me see now, erm yes, erm…the planet is divided into various areas called countries; each one is ruled over by a king, queen, or a dictator; then there are prime ministers and presidents as well," John rattled off whilst masticating his way through yet another of his favoured sandwiches, knowing most of it anyway having taken the subject recently in boarding school.

"It can be a dangerous world but there are some fantastic and mind-blowing places, not to mention loads of brilliant creatures like lions, tigers, elephants and others…"

There was no comment at all from the alien entity squatting in the mind of its young human host, not that John was particularly minded as he continued chewing and talking at the same time.

"There are huge sprawling tropical forests and enormous sandy deserts, then there's the Great Wall of China, the Grand Canyon, the Great Barrier Reef, massive oceans, fiery volcanoes…"

Again the off-world being remained silent listening to the food-devouring human child running through a veritable compendium of landmarks on his own home planet.

"Very high mountains rising into the skies, pyramids, tropical fishes of all kinds and colours, lots and lots more, that's if we don't destroy the planet first."

"Destroy the planet first? I find it difficult to understand your meaning, John Philips. Why would human beings want to destroy the very planet they need to survive on?" The bemused extra-terrestrial currently housed in his head voiced, the alien unable to comprehend such blatantly unforgivable stupidity from a population that should love their host planet like a god not want to destroy it.

"Survival of the dominant species must always take priority without fail, otherwise chaos ensues. In what way were humanity to do such an abominable deed?"

"I…er…I don't know. Mum and dad are always reading about atom bombs or global warming, draughts and famines, and meteorites from outer space wiping us out. It doesn't look good, does it?" The unsmiling boy proffered finishing the sandwich and wondering if he could manage another; deciding instead not to and reached for the giant bottle of lemonade.

"Not really, your race faces extinction indeed if what you tell me is true, John Philips. Then again, solar flares from your own star could burn the planet up equally easily," responded the vibrating voice from another world deep at the back of his brain, its knowledge far in advance of his own, but he was more than willing to learn.

"Although the chances of it actually happening are quite slim, no one wants to witness the demise of the two-legged pleasure creatures. We like your eco world as it is."

"Pleasure creatures? I don't understand."

"Your species lives for pleasure, physical as well as spiritual as far as I can ascertain, capable of loving, hating, and inflicting pain and fear to each other and all of the indigenous creatures," confessed his non-human passenger matter of factly as its host took a long gulp of lemonade from the plastic bottle he was holding, his mind reeling from the information pouring in.

"You are mentally closed to the other races of intellectually superior, inter-dimensionally challenged life forms both in and around the multiverses beyond your comprehension."

"Mul…multiverses! I've been taught about the multiverses but no one has ever mentioned any multiverses. Is it anything to do with calculus?" The befuddled boy quizzed, burping loudly then apologising out of habit, something completely alien to the extra-terrestrial alien listening on in his head.

"Ah yes, calculus, the branch of your mathematics concerned with the effect on a function of an infinitesimal change in the independent variable. Hmm, not at all," informed the inner voice with a knowledgeable certainty, its tone suddenly changing in pitch having again utilised his host's senses on hearing unidentifiable noises close by the house.

"Wait! Quick, John Philips, with secrecy and stealth in mind, I want you to get up and take a very careful peek out of the front and back windows so that we can identify what is happening out there." Urged on by the alien entity, he stood up and strolled over to the window, then gingerly peeled back the curtain, being careful not to make it twitch visibly from outside.

There was nothing moving at all out at the back of the house as he peered all around the various back gardens, only to suddenly catch sight of something over to his far left.

They saw it together, a small group of camouflage-uniformed soldiers were busy searching the rear quadrangle of garden sheds and all, including his own to try and find them.

"Yes, yes, I see them as you do. Be careful and check the front of your dwelling, John Philips," barked the anxious-sounding voice, forcing him to do just that. John eased the curtain back into place, then turned and padded out of the room to do likewise from the upstairs landing window.

"As I predicted, they are scouring the entire town in order to find me and you. Are all of the points of entry and exit locked and sealed?"

"Yes, they are. The only way in would be for them to break in and I don't think they would do that. Do you?" The frowning boy bleated as he stared out at the sea of soldiers searching high and low for both him and the clever alien entity currently housed in his brain.

"No, John Philips, not unless they suspect that we are inside, so I suggest that we deposit ourselves back in the rear room we were originally in and remain as quiet as possible," responded the unphased extra-terrestrial hoping to calm the boy's jangling nerves and succeeding as well with the rest of his words of wisdom music to his ears in the circumstances.

"Do not move around but adopt a stationary position and do not utter a single sound aloud just in case they are utilising noise and movement detecting apparatus; remember not a single sound."

They did just that. John turned and tip-toed back to his own bedroom. Once there, he sat down on the carpet to begin the silent motionless period as mentioned by his makeshift soulmate.

Apart from the dangers they faced from the searching soldiers milling around outside the house, there was also the possibility of him getting a cramp or sneezing as well to think about.

It was made that much more palatable by his being able to talk to the ship-jumping alien in his head via his own thoughts rendering speaking aloud unnecessary.

"H…how long will we have to stay here for, any guess?" The pensive boy asked sprawled out on the orange bedroom carpet, his inner thoughts instantly answered by the ever-attentive alien straining to decipher the noises from outside as well.

"Perhaps for a further twenty of your Earth minutes, then we can check on their progress and proximity; that is if they have not heard us first, John Philips," proffered his extra-terrestrial companion over the sounds of door knobs being turned and windows banged on from close by; even the coal houses and garden sheds and greenhouses were checked.

"I haven't heard anyone's house getting broken into; not yet anyway."

"They obviously do not know who you are, John Philips, otherwise they would have already broken in and taken us away by now," replied the voice having suddenly leapt from the back of his head to the frontal lobe, irritatingly so, mused John to himself as the entity continued to vibrate annoyingly as it spoke.

"But if they ever do discover your true identity and address, they will be back to do just that. What we need is another of your safe hiding places."

"Well, there are a number of places we could go, but when?" John admitted having run his thoughts over several possible places he knew were known to no one but him and his pals, only for ET to once again put his nose out of joint.

"Hmm, yes, Bank Terrace tree tops a possibility, storm drains a bit difficult to flee from if discovered, cliff top caravan might topple off, old farm may well be easier to…"

"Hey, hey, those are my own special places, not yours, only I am supposed to know them."

John almost said out loud stopping himself just in time to think it instead, something noted upon immediately by the friendly but concerned alien entity listening on.

"Do not say it out loud, John Philips, or they might pick up on it with their technology. They are at this dwelling's portals as we speak," groaned his otherworld alter ego admonishing him for almost giving the game away and getting them both caught; something he already realised he'd nearly succeeded in doing.

"If they do not suspect that we are here, they will try the portal handles then move on to the next dwelling along and we can return to our discussion."

"I hope so, I really do," whimpered a truly nervous John Philips, who sat fearing the worst; his inner fears were picked up on by the experienced alien entity hoping that the young human child would not give them away.

"Remain calm, John Philips, we must convince them that we are not inside this dwelling place, then once the sun has departed the sky, we will find my starship, yes," informed his concerned co-pilot doing his level best to placate the uncomfortable boy, whose inability to control his emotions may well get them both captured or worse.

"That still leaves us over half a day to play with before it begins to get dark," John enthused to the friendly off-world entity having realised that the house had not been broken into as they suspected it to have been. They were in the clear for now.

"By then, we shouldn't have any trouble leaving here and making our way down to the park. You'll be back in that spaceship and up into outer space in no time at all."

"You said you had something for me, Mister Cavenaugh, I am in the mood to be impressed," enthused an unsmiling General Smithlington hovering over the number 4 computer console, having been summoned there by an ever-efficient Greg Cavenaugh hopefully with some very good news for him.

"I've cracked it. What we've got here, General, is a John James Philips, a twelve year old boy whose family lives right here in the town at number 6 Trinity Road."

"A twelve year old boy eh, I don't think we will have too much trouble finding and detaining him. Well done, Mister Cavanaugh," responded a supremely confident-sounding General Smithlington with a clap of his large hands, the big officer was impressed with the result, even though the town had already been searched from top to bottom with no sign of their target.

"Get that information over to the search teams and tell them to pay a surprise visit to that address and collect our guests."

"Right away, General."

"On that most delicious of note, the rest of you might as well begin packing all this equipment away; next stop, the local park and the spaceship itself," boomed the beaming army officer, having successfully achieved the task of locating the troublesome young boy and with him the ET they so sorely wanted to get their hands on.

"We may need that alien creature to help open the doors into the thing we've been trying to secure for many long years. It'll be dark soon and that will play them right into our soldiers' clutches; it can't miss."

Chapter Four

"John Philips! John Philips! JOHN PHILIPS!"

"Wh…wha…what is it?" The bleary-eyed boy drawled, having been rather rudely awoken by the loud voice in his own head as the alien interloper hailed him from the deep sleep he'd fallen into.

"It is as I feared, they know we are here. They are close by disturbingly so and will quickly surround this domicile of yours. We need to leave straight away whilst we can."

The sheer panic in the alien's tone of voice was there for him to hear, forcing the still fully dressed boy to climb off the bed and hurry out to the upstairs landing window.

Without disturbing the curtains, he took a careful peek outside, almost immediately catching sight of at least six army vehicles' lights switched off and disgorging soldiers.

"What are we going to do? We could hide but if we do, they may well tear my parents' house down trying to find us."

"No, John Philips, we have got to leave here as soon and as quietly as we can. Now, John Philips, now!" An equally uncomfortable alien entity urged its shrill words of warning instantly hitting home and forcing him to remember a long-used emergency exit from the house known only to him.

"I know a way out and we might just make it away from here if we are lucky," hissed a suddenly wide-awake John Philips, turning and sprinting back into his bedroom, grabbing the pencil torch whilst jumping onto his bed and reaching for the curtains.

Without bothering about anyone possibly looking on from outside, he yanked the curtains wide open whilst flicking up the thin metal catch on the larger of the right-hand windows.

With speed the only priority, John pushed the big window fully open, then climbed out, lowering himself down onto the family shed roof immediately below.

Instead of diving for cover, the knowledgeable boy turned and reached back up to ease the window into a closed position, seeing the latch fall and click shut again.

"Yes, yes, John Philips, seal it back up so as to make the men pursuing us believe that we are still there in hiding thus giving us time to get away, clever boy."

Knowing full well that they had scant seconds to make their escape. John fell flat on his belly and began a snake-like wriggle along the flat shed roof.

Instead of heading for his own back garden, he made for that of their next-door neighbour's to his right having already decided on a preplanned escape route to freedom.

On reaching the very edge, he swivelled around hundred and eighty degrees, then began to lower himself over the side, dangling down by his hands before releasing his grip and dropping to the ground below.

"Well done so far, John Philips, what now?" The equally wantaway alien voice inside the head of the wind tousled boy gushed, who already knew what he had in mind and was in mid-sprint as he answered the question.

"This is what I'm doing now; here goes nothing."

With cat-like agility, he leapt forward and straddled, then jumped the waist-high hedge in one easy movement, crunching painfully down on the other side on a newly concreted patio garden.

"OW! Damn them! This was grass the last time I did that."

"Keep moving, John Philips, we need to be undercover and out of sight," droned the pesky extra-terrestrial visitor to planet Earth with complete disregard for the condition and pain the boy was suffering at that particular moment in time.

"Y…yes, we can sneak away through the vegetable garden, ouch!" On saying that, John climbed to his feet and started a low loping run over to and on into his near neighbour's upper veg garden, getting as far as the corn on the cob plants only for a movement to catch his and the alien's eye.

"Quickly, John Philips, go before we are noticed!" The startled voice hissed on catching sight of a tall dark shape silhouetted against the white rear garden fence, visible thanks to a full moon popping out from behind the clouds.

John was already flying through the air like an acrobatic goalkeeper long before the final word was spoken having seen the gun-toting soldier at the same moment.

As luck would have it, he landed reasonably soundlessly atop a mound of discarded washing lines and gardening clothing. John was unable to suppress a pained yell, only nothing came out.

"H…hey what happened? Noth…nothing came out?"

"Sorry, John Philips, but I momentarily took over the control of your larynx just in case, the right thing in the circumstances," replied his guardian alien angel as the mystified boy lay face down in an unmoving heap, his mind reeling at what he had just been told.

"Did he hear me fall?" A troubled John Philips asked from his horizontal position in the midst of his neighbour's crop of corn on the cob plants having leapt away from danger a moment earlier.

"Affirmative, John Philips, we have escaped detection for now but must continue onwards whilst we can."

They heard it together, the sound of a door being forced open, his door back at number 6. They had gone in to find him. It was time to go.

"Go, John Philips, they have violated your family's domicile and are even now searching for us. We have to go, NOW," snapped his suddenly agitated alien extra-terrestrial mind guest, both of them increasingly desperate to flee from possible detection and capture once the entire house had been searched.

John needed no second warning having already clambered to his feet and sprinted hard for the other side of the garden, leaping easily over a low brick wall like a startled gazelle.

"Run, John Philips, get us to safety and me back into my own space vessel. We have to put as much distance between them and us before they realise that we have tricked them," boomed the nervously jittery entity as an equally uncomfortable John ran for his life, the sprinting boy feeling slightly uneasy and disorientated as the alien flitted from zone to zone in his head.

"Don't…don't move around so much in there, will you? I can't con…concentrate," groaned the groggy boy clambering over a high wooden fence and almost falling, thanks to the anxious alien moving through areas of his brain like a nervous prisoner in his cell.

"Sorry about that but hurry, John Philips, we do not have too much time before all Zobodiah breaks loose back there and they call in the dreaded helicopter to seek us out," squawked the clearly worried alien, deciding to settle in his frontal lobe where it could keep a close watch on events from its human counterparts own senses area.

"Zobo…Zobodiah you…you said 'all Zobodiah breaks loose'? Wha…what did you mean?"

"We will discuss it on another occasion but now, we have to go from this place or face the consequences."

John took the hint remaining silent whilst concentrating instead on trying to remember the exact layout of the next garden along as he hauled himself over a high brick wall to find his feet ankle-deep in a newly built pond.

With soldiers wearing infrared night-vision, they had a very real advantage over him, yet he knew the town and housing estate like the back of his hand, an advantage to him they didn't have.

A panting John finally made it to the sixth garden along and the escape exit of his choosing when a high-pitched whistle sent an icy shiver up and down his spine.

"They have discovered our subterfuge. Hurry, John Philips, we do not have much time, RUN!" The unnerved otherworldly being boomed from inside his brain as the realisation that the soldiers had quickly found that their young target had fled the scene hit him hard.

Yes, run, he told himself turning and sprinting towards where he hoped was the mid-terraced house communal passageway which like his own one, allowed access from the back garden to the front of both buildings.

A moment later, he was running hard into and through the passage hearing his footsteps echoing slightly in the claustrophobically enclosed confines as he did so.

"Yes, left and up to Ranby Drive, I see, I see, hurry we must evade capture," droned the mind-reading alien passenger as he exited the passageway into the cool night air. John found it mentally draining having to find his way in almost total darkness, then he remembered his torch.

"No light at all, John Philips, we are still too close to those seeking our whereabouts."

He heard the entity tell him whilst running across a rectangular local green towards a wide gap in a waist-high roadside hedge, only to misjudge it badly and fall over it instead.

It was a horribly painful mistake as the confident boy flew up and over in a rip of clothing and agonised grunt, thudding down on the wet grass on the other side.

"You appear to have no physical injuries perhaps several dermis abrasions; rise and run, John Philips, straight away."

John was in no mood for a lecture on his aching body but he did see sense in not laying there feeling sorry for himself in the face of the very real danger facing them both.

Climbing slowly to his feet, he was about to begin running again when he, and through him, the entity caught sight of a series of flashing lights and instantly knew what they were.

"Th…that's them, isn't it?" The panting boy wheezed, seemingly mesmerised by the swiftly moving flickers of light heading their way, his temporary halt quickly picked up on by a wantaway extra-terrestrial.

"Yes, it is they, and they will soon be upon us if we linger here, John Philips, we have to get closer to my vessel. Run, go."

The startled boy needed no second reminder of their vulnerability what with soldiers wearing infrared night-vision searching high and low for them they were still sitting ducks.

Turning and running hard in a direction he knew to be due south, he quickly reached a junction and took the left turn off the main road. Then they heard a frighteningly familiar sound.

"Tha…that's a heli…heli…heli."

"Helicopter! Yes, John Philips, and not too far away if I am not mistaken. If they have ultraviolet capabilities, they will be able to witness our movements with ease," responded the alien voice in his head cutting off the stammering Earthling boy and utilising his senses to vastly increase his own in order to better gauge the distances involved.

"Think, my human friend. Have you a place to hide in nearer to my ship? We have the advantage over them in that they do not know which direction we have taken. Think."

John did just that, running and thinking, finding his thoughts suddenly disturbingly blank as far as local hiding places were concerned as tiredness took its toll.

"I…erm, the…there is a place, now let me think."

"Think quicker, John Philips, because once that helicopter seeks us out, they will reveal our location to everyone and they will set up a net for us to run into. Well?"

"I've got it! The very place. Once we get there, we'll be safe there to plan a way to get you to your spaceship."

"Get us there, John Philips, run as fast as your two human legs can go. We must not get caught," drawled a nervy alien in his head knowing as he did that he was in good company with this particular human child and if anyone could outfox its armed elders, he could; he had to.

"You heard me correctly, Colonel, we've missed the boy but only just, he must have seen us approaching and fled the house," informed a slightly nervous Captain Jack Stainger as he stood gazing out through the missing boy's bedroom window having led his men into the house only to come up empty-handed.

"Damn him! Damn them both! Hopefully, the search chopper will soon pick the boy up, it'll be with you any moment now," voiced a furious Colonel Smithlington following the news that they had somehow allowed the alien housing boy to elude the team of crack professional soldiers as easily as he had done.

"At least we do know that the ET will want the boy to take it back to its spaceship and that will be its undoing. Let the pilot know that I need him to find that boy, no excuses."

"How's it going with the alien's flying saucer, Sir, if you don't mind my asking?" An already under the cosh Captain Stainger asked having managed to lose the errant boy and with him the much sought-after alien visitor; he was on very thin ice indeed.

"We have successfully transported it to the local Hall Garth Park where we hope to gain access to its interior in the not too distant future," announced Colonel Smithlington matter of factly, his tone one of irked annoyance aimed solely at the officer on the other end of the telephone as did his comments.

"Mind you, if I could find an officer clever enough to catch a small child, it would make my bloody day as indeed you were meant to do, Captain Stainger."

"Don't worry, Colonel, we'll bring the kid to you; it's only a matter of time that's all. Hey, I think that's the helicopter now. I'll keep you posted, bye for now."

"Yes, I certainly hope you do find him because, at this moment in time, I doubt whether you could find your arse cheeks with both cupped hands. Get that boy, Captain, or else."

On saying that, the line went dead in his ear, leaving the embarrassed captain even more determined to find and capture the ET-hosting child than ever before.

Thumping his right fist down hard on the window sill in anger, the miffed captain utilised the army frequency lapel intercom to call his team sergeant to get an instant update.

"How are we doing out there, Plarshore? Have you got him yet?"

"Er, not yer, Captain, but the chopper has arrived, any instructions for the pilot at all?" A slightly breathless Sergeant Bernard Plarshore replied as he leapt over yet another garden fence and again struggled to keep his footing on landing whilst taking the call.

"Why is it so fucking difficult to find a small fucking boy? Well, Sergeant?" His fiercesome superior officer snapped via his lapel comm unit; the captain's voice tinged with barely disguised fury obviously having been chewed out himself by those higher in the chain.

"We are doing our utmost to get him but it would help if we knew which direction he went in, Sir."

"Start working your team eastwards towards the town's Hall Garth Park and tell the chopper pilot to do likewise and remember that the boy knows Hornsea a damn sight better than we do," volunteered a snarling Captain Stainger turning and walking out of the bedroom and down the stairs to join his team outside; they needed all the help they could get out there.

The young boy was clever, perhaps too clever, mused the confident captain whilst strolling towards the wide open back door and out into the darkness, slipping his infrared device on as he went.

It was a small seaside town with only a certain amount of places that the boy and alien guest could go to try and avoid the search helicopter's ultraviolet heat and motion detectors.

Then once detected, they'll quickly be picked up, locked away, and then turned over to the boffins to work on; from there the ET and its technology will be well and truly in human hands.

Whether that would be good or not was not his to say, he was only a soldier obeying orders; his conscience was clear but he couldn't speak for anyone else.

"It…it's alright. We…we should be fairly safe here. No one knows about this place but me and a few of my friends. It's our den, if you follow my drift," gushed a breathless John with an element of pride in his voice as he sat cross-legged at the foot of a four foot deep, wood-lined square hole he himself had helped to excavate.

Thanks largely to his best friend's father, it was concealed by an ingenious winch and pulley system that made a long length of wood fit snugly in place hiding it from all but them.

"I assume that by 'den', you are alluding to a place for hiding away for cogitative endeavours," replied the knowledgeable alien entity lodged deep in his brain. It seemed to know things it had no right gaining access to, seeming to use its mind to cross reference information it required.

"You can't possibly know that. Who told you?"

"You yourself told me; our minds are interlinked so I can access it at will so to speak. You cannot do so to me because my own physical brain is still aboard my ship," volunteered the inner alternative voice now suddenly at the very back of his brain, annoyingly so, as if searching for something, perhaps a stray thought or memory he'd hidden away.

"I also am able to ascertain that this is something of a nest of sorts, a second home in which to dodge other children of your age and kind."

John did not reply straight away. He felt slightly embarrassed at the level of personal intrusion; something the alien entity was quick to pick up on.

"I don't mind it too much but what do we do if they catch us?"

"We must not entertain that notion, John Philips. Get me to my vessel and we will both be free to go our separate ways," reeled off the uncomfortably situated voice now at the very centre of his brain again as it responded to the question it found to be unthinkable in the extreme.

"We can't stay here forever, when do we set off again?" John wanted to know, and suddenly liked the idea of ridding himself of the annoyingly irritating alien entity lodged deep in his own brain.

"We have made it so far, John Philips, perhaps it is time to get going. We cannot utilise the conventional routes and therefore must get there via another method," ventured the eager alien desperate to reach its ship and escape the blue-green third planet from the sun once and for all, out into the far reaches of space.

"Do you know of any other alternate ways that will avoid those pursuing us, my trusty human child? I assume that you do."

"Er, yes and no. I do know one or two different ways of us getting to the park unseen but we will still have to cross that main road leading to the beach, I can't avoid it."

His answer seemed to silence the usually talkative unflappable alien entity as it mulled over their situation and any possible alternatives to the predicament they found themselves in.

"We will just have to risk discovery but I ask you to utilise all of your courage, local knowledge, and experience to outwit those hoping to catch us, help me get there please, Earth boy."

"I…I'll do my best. I can't do any more. Why don't I take a quick look out to see if the coast is clear?"

"The coast, John Philips? Surely the coast is over to the east precisely point seven of your Earth miles from here," quizzed the strange voice in his head as the off-earthly alien attempted to ascertain exactly what the boy had meant by what was clearly an erroneous statement.

"No, no, it's got nothing to do with the actual coast, it is a saying. I think it comes from ancient nautical times when ships smuggled contraband ashore," garbled the blustering boy hoping that his explanation was making sense to the alien entity listening on.

"Or maybe it's for ships leaving harbours checking that no enemy shipping was out there waiting for them. We use it as very much the same thing. Is there anybody out there, you know?"

"Thank you, John Philips. Yes, let's check that the coast is indeed clear. I will be your eyes and ears," volunteered his equally want away extra-terrestrial entity, moving swiftly across to his sensory area so as to superenhance both his eyesight and hearing.

They did just that as John gingerly pushed open the long panel and peered out into the surrounding blackness. Together, they looked and listened in all directions.

They remained there for fully a minute, the alien entity making doubly certain that the coast really was clear as the Earth boy had termed it. It was.

"The vicinity is clear of other humans, let us go. Which way, John Philips?" The voice prompted once satisfied that there were no infrared-wearing soldiers anywhere in the area having quickly handed the vital sense areas to the boy he was addressing.

"Hang on whilst I get my bearings, we'll be better off cutting across the country from here," ventured the slightly disorientated boy, not particularly enjoying having to move around in the pitch blackness, even though he knew the area like the back of his hand in daylight.

"First, let me recover my den so that it'll remain invisible to adults or anyone else for that matter. Right then, let's go."

The den was constructed on a piece of wasteland around the side of a row of mainly unused garages on Ebor Avenue playing fields but all looked weirdly different without street lamps.

Without a second thought, he ran to his left heading for a gap in a nearby fence backing onto a bushy hedgerow, behind a set of children's swings and a roundabout.

"We must keep checking for lights and the helicopter as we go, John Philips, they will be closely scrutinising this location in every effort to find you, then me," enthused the alien voice in his brain as he ducked into the gap, only to miss it entirely, running smack bang into the fence and ending up sprawled out on his back for his troubles.

"OW! Damn it! Sorry, I seem to have misjudged it," groaned a seriously embarrassed John. The shaken boy clambered back up onto his feet more frustrated than anything else having missed the gap altogether.

Once he'd dusted himself down, he tried again, this time feeling for the gap first before rushing headlong through it, finding himself in a fairly recently ploughed field.

"We are out in the open with nowhere to hide, John Philips, run towards some trees or bushes if indeed there are any," snapped his flustered mind co-pilot as an equally unnerved John ran hard for the solitary detached building he knew stood on the very bottom corner by the main road.

"Wha…what's that sound?" The sprinting boy spluttered via burning lungs where the soft wet mud underfoot forced him to work even harder whilst deep wave-like furrows continually tripped and hampered his progress.

"The helicopter! It can only be the helicopter! Find us some cover, Earthling boy, before they get a fix on us."

"I…I think I know somewhere, if…if it's still there; keep your fingers crossed," gasped John whilst leaping gazelle-like over horribly undulating gulleys of freshly cultivated soil determined to keep him from reaching his destination and safety.

"The flying vessel is approximately seventy-four seconds away from picking up our ultraviolet body heat. Go, John Philips, go."

"Sev…seve…seventy f…f…"

"I suggest you concentrate on running and not speaking, John Philips, do not trip and fall or we will be in trouble."

A moment later, he did just that, tripping then falling, rolling over and over across several furrows before coming to a stop in one of the shallow grave-like trenches.

"Aargh! Oh shredded wheat! They are going to find us now, aren't they?" A thoroughly dejected John exclaimed, lying sprawled out in the middle of the muddy cultivated field; the helicopter still approaching now only half a minute away.

"Hmm maybe not, reach out and feel the harder soil at the top of the furrow in front of us; go on, John Philips," urged the alien entity whilst relocating to other areas of his brain so as to feel it as well.

"As I thought, very well compacted yet still malleable, I am about to take control of your muscular abilities. Do not be afraid, it is for the best."

On saying that, John suddenly felt himself go slightly groggy as the knowledgeable entity took him over, reaching over and tugging hard at the heaped peak of cultivated furrow above him.

Using strength, agility, and know-how he never knew he possessed, he found himself gripping and heaving at an area of sliced earth at an astonishing speed.

In a matter of moments, he heaved, manipulated, and shaped a rough mud cocoon around him, not totally encasing him but enough to hide his body heat from above.

By bashing the inner wall extremely hard, he managed to thin it enough to bend but remain intact. It was not perfect but it might just do the trick.

"It is done, the flying machine is here, John Philips, we shall soon see whether my ministering has proved successful or not." He heard the voice reveal as he returned to his own senses, only to find himself encased in a coil of shiny earth, his body cold and shivering as he lay listening.

They heard it together, rotor blades sounding as the helicopter circled the detached house close by and then detoured over the field they were hidden in.

"They are leaving! We are successful, John Philips, but we do not have time to remain here; your troops will soon be arriving. Time to move onwards."

As if on cue, the icy cold boy began a wriggling forward motion, quickly crawling free from the damp-smelling cocoon of mud made somehow by the alien hiding in his head.

"How…how did you learn to do that?" The quizzical boy stammered whilst climbing to his feet and turning to see the unusual handiwork, only to stare into utter blackness, he could see nothing at all.

"There is no time to explain. I will tell you once we are safe from discovery. The helicopter will soon return; start running, John Philips," informed the desperately wanted away entity feeling incredibly vulnerable standing out in the middle of a ploughed field with no cover anywhere in sight.

John took the hint, starting a strong sprint down in the direction of the main coast road heading for the open field beyond and the hiding places it would hopefully afford them.

"Whe…where's the helicopter right now?" John wheezed as he continued running towards the road, now quite close to it but not a hundred per cent certain of exactly where it was, and slowing slightly just in case.

"The flying machine is currently out of range but I suspect that those searching on foot are very close; we need to leave this area altogether."

At that moment, a flash of brilliant white light lit up the entire single detached house as one of the oncoming super trooper mounted land rovers approached the foot of the hill.

"They have us, John Philips, they have us. There is nowhere to hide!" The panic-stricken alien entity shrieked on catching sight of the vehicle about to round the corner and fix them fully in its powerful spotlight.

"They haven't got us yet, hold on," growled the panting boy, not knowing the word 'defeat', not whilst he had his wits about him. John used the bright light to gauge the distance between him and the roadside fence.

Suddenly, he dived forward full length sliding to a halt, then shuffling as close as possible to the lowest horizontal across beam and lay as still as he possibly could.

"What are you doing, John Philips? They will easily locate us."

"Trust me, there's at least nine inches at the bottom, they'll drive straight on by without seeing us."

It took what seemed ages as the land rover trundled its way along and eventually passed the trembling boys' hiding place, spewing brilliant light in its wake.

"There! I told you so. Once we get across the road, we will be out of danger, okay," proffered a jubilant John Philips, standing up and peering after the receding land rover about to disappear around the corner and on to the seafront.

"Wait a moment, John Philips, whilst I check that we are still safe from scrutiny via your own senses."

John stood peering the other way as the alien entity took over his powers of hearing and sight, maximising them via its abilities so as to check events behind them.

"We are lucky at this particular moment that they have not quite reached the corner. Let us go, John Philips."

Seconds later, things returned to normal as far as his senses were concerned and he clambered his way through the fence and then ran across the unlit main road.

Following several painful attempts to find a way through the straggly hawthorn and elderberry bushes making up the undergrowth, he finally entered the field beyond.

Even though he knew the stream dyke field like the back of his hand in daylight, now in complete and utter darkness, it was an accident waiting to happen, frighteningly so.

Digging deep into his memory banks, John turned ninety degrees right and began a slow jog keeping the bushy undergrowth at that side as he went.

The field itself was mostly knee-length grass divided in two by a stream running diagonally across it and backed by the long disused ex-railway line cinder track.

A single muddy pathway also ran diagonally across it as a shortcut from the council estate to the town centre, the road shielded from view via a narrow grassy track John was now on.

"It is extremely dark here, John Philips, so I will attempt to go to your sight centres and allow as much light in as allowed. Do not be alarmed," voiced the alien lodged deep in his brain; its plan hopefully one he would like to have happen as the risk of his getting a branch in the eye or toppling over was a very real danger.

Suddenly, his way ahead grew slightly in intensity, only by a small amount but a definite help as the alien reminded him of the dangers facing them.

"We have company, John Philips; the helicopter is returning so I suggest you find a suitable hiding place before they find us with their technology aids."

"Damn it! The…there's a place just up ahead if it's not been blocked up," retorted the panicking boy suddenly cocking an ear skywards to try and hear the sound of rotor blades, only for several bright flashes of light behind the foliage to catch his attention.

"Yes, John Philips, the next searching vehicle is coming, we must get under cover before they get to us."

"Thanks to you, I can tell where I am a little bit better. There is a pipe just up ahead feeding water down a tiny gulley down to the stream; it's there we can hide."

"The under-road feed pipe, yes, very clever, John Philips," volunteered his alien admirer picking his brain in a way he did not like particularly; still there wasn't time to worry about it now of all times.

"We have approximately fifty seconds before the helicopter will be almost on top of us. Do something, my clever human friend."

With the alien's words ringing in his ears, John tripped, finding himself sliding headlong through the long grass and down into a ditch, head first before quickly scrambling upright again.

"We haven't got time for fun and games, John Philips, we have to hide and now!"

"Eeurgh! Oh shit, I'm sorry! Hey, we're there! This is it, my hiding place, er there, in there. Look, ow! Stinging nettles, ow!" A spluttering John yelled feeling himself on hands and knees in several inches of icy cold water and a patch of stinging nettles just as the helicopter came into view.

"They are here, John Philips. Do something, hide us!"

John was already pushing and kicking his wet, aching body back as hard as he could, furiously back peddling, forcing both legs in through foliage and cobwebs alike.

In a matter of seconds, he had jammed himself horizontally into the icy cold pipe, gripping the outer edge with frozen fingers as the helicopter circled the field.

"We seem to have made it just in time, John Philips, but I fear that those searching for us on two feet will soon be upon us," the relieved alien informed him as a cramp began twinging in his left calf muscle, not that he could do anything about it squeezed as he was into a tightly confined space.

"As I said, they haven't got us yet. Once that thing flies away, we'll slip hopefully unnoticed down to the stream dyke; from there, the rest will be easy," grunted a grimacing John Philips as the pain became virtually unbearable, forcing the clever alien entity to help him, easing it all together in the process.

"Hey, it's gone. What did you do?" The wet, nettle-stung, thorn-ripped boy inquired as the feeling of cramp suddenly vanished altogether, leaving him pondering on how it had happened.

"I simply readjusted your pain threshold and barrier so that you can will it away."

"You will have to show me how you do that sometimes, I could make a fortune with such a talent," ventured a pain-free John Philips still wedged inside the cold, wet pipe listening to the sound of rotor blades and catching sight of flashes of bright light as well.

"Yes, perhaps I will but for now, the helicopter appears to be heading west. We should be setting off to my vessel now before they get any closer."

His alien counterpart was right as far as it being time to go was concerned as he began the task of heaving and hauling himself out of the tightly unforgiving pipe.

Once fully free of its confines, he decided it best to remain in the tiny trickling gulley and began a low lopping walk along and down its grass and weed-strewn depths.

The helicopter could still be heard but was now back at the estate no doubt double-checking that they had not overlooked the boy at all.

Suddenly, the entire length of the viaduct passage was lit up as the next land rover along shone its powerful super trooper in the direction they were heading.

"Remain as still as you can, John Philips, we are covered by the tall grasses around us, we will be quite safe for now," informed the alien in his head as the area up ahead illuminated like never before as their searchers peered down the hill using infrared night-vision to aid them.

Seconds later, all was dark again as those within the land rover satisfied themselves that all was clear and drove on leaving its shivering quarry to do likewise.

"Let us continue, John Philips, get me to my craft before your people get to me."

Without bothering to reply, John resumed the same bent backed lope of earlier slowly getting ever closer to the stream and the concrete bridge spanning it.

"Where do we go once we reach this stream of yours?"

The ever-vigilant alien entity wanted to know as once again a long beam of light flashed its way across the entire grassy field as the helicopter signalled its return.

"ZZSOPOOGREEAALS! That helicopter is returning. Sorry about the bad language, John Philips, but we need to hide again. Have you got a place to do so?"

"Und…under the bridge, it's our only chance," growled a disappointed John Philips; the soaked bedraggled boy forgetting the discomfort he felt in favour of running the final few metres instead.

A quick lookup told him that the helicopter was heading for the dyke itself and would no doubt follow it all the way along its length, catching them as it did so.

On reaching the bridge, he decided it best to jump out of the ditch and quickly run across the narrow tarmac pathway so as to avoid being seen by the oncoming helicopter.

"What are you thinking, John Philips? We might be seen by them on infrared night-vision," squawked an alarmed alien entity as they sprinted into possible view of all of their pursuers; surely it was not the thing to do in the circumstances.

"We have got no choice with the helicopter flying straight at us, they will see us for certain if we go under on that side."

John's reply silenced the panic-stricken extra-terrestrial at once as it mentally weighed up the logic involved in the human child's thinking.

With the helicopter aiming for them, the desperate boy ducked down the side, nearly knocking himself out in the process as he scraped the concrete wall in the blackness.

In his hurry to dodge those aboard the speeding helicopter, he forgot to slow down as he ran down the side of the bridge, slipping on thick mud and actually ending up in the water as a result.

"EEOURGH! Oogh! Damn it, I'm all wet! Shit!"

"Get out of the water as fast as you can, your ripples will be seen by them. NOW, John Philips!" The outraged alien yelled realising at once what would happen to the disturbed water once the ripples exited the bridge on either side any moment now if he remained there.

John did just that, clambering and scrambling back up and out of the brackish black water, slipping down again on the muddy bank and cursing at his bad fortune.

By the time he was on his feet again, the helicopter was overhead hovering momentarily but not stopping much to the delight and relief as they heard then saw it fly onwards.

"They'll never find us under here, not in a million years," bleated a confident-sounding, mud-caked, soaking wet John Philips as he leaned back against one of several support pillars holding the concrete bridge in place.

"A valuable lesson, John Philips, never underestimate your own species. You are a crafty, intelligent, curious civilisation; not all but most of you," countered his locked-in extra-terrestrial lodger as they stood chewing the fat whilst the hunt for them continued to gather pace and momentum all around.

"I suppose we are quite interesting, we Earthlings, wouldn't you say?" The shivering cold, soaking wet boy warbled as the helicopter did an about turn and headed back along the stream towards them just as voices sounded in the field close by.

"Yes, I agree but right now, we must find a way to distract that flying machine so that we can leave this place without being seen at all. Think, John Philips, think," blurted the alien entity as the searching ground troops came ever closer to their hiding place with all the consequences it implied to them both.

"Ther…there might be a way, but I need a stone, preferably a round flat one. Now let me see…" replied a confident John Philips as a rudimentary plan emerged in his overcrowded mind; one that might just work if his luck held, and it had to for both their sakes.

"Duck disturbing? We haven't got time to play games, John Philips, we have to get away from here as soon as possible," challenged the quizzical ET, not quite grasping what the boy had fully in mind as John searched desperately for the right shape and sized stones from the muddy bank underfoot.

"It's not a game, not if it works. It should work a treat if I get it right. Aah, what have we here," proffered John whilst raking his wet fingers into and through the thick mud and coming up with a few suitably flattish stones, washing the worst of the dirt off them in the icy stream.

"Yes, these feel about right. Now how far away is that flaming helicopter, can you work it out for me?"

"Judging from the sound and light display, I would say that it's arcing back this way, John Philips."

"Good! Good! Here goes nothing…"

On saying that, the determined boy edged his way to the very end of the bridge, then with one hand holding on for balance, aimed then threw a stone at where he hoped was the estate side bank.

It failed and nothing happened so he tried again. This time he attempted to skim it along the top of the water, listening as it crashed into the reed bed, disturbing something in the process.

Success was sweet as one or perhaps two ducks came flapping and squawking out of hiding and half flew, half swam away in the other direction seeking alternate sleeping arrangements.

"YES! Let's hope they were spotted by the crew inside the helicopter. Hey yes, they turned the lamp down onto the stream. What do you think?"

"Well done, John Philips, but let's use it to our advantage, shall we? Let's get going."

The alien entity was right and he knew it as he began a delicate waddle across the muddy bank to the opposite side and from there into the long wet grasses lining the stream itself.

"We've got quite a head-start on them but for how long," mumbled John turning back to see what was happening and seeing a large group of men silhouetted in the bright beam of light thrown down from the helicopter hovering over their heads.

"Don't look a gift horse in the mouth, my clever Earthling boy, the further from them, the safer I will feel," groaned his alien sidekick in the brain department, wondering just where they were in relation to his spaceship at all. The boy had to get him there, he had to…

"Tell me, John Philips, are we still heading for your village's Hall Garth Park and my vessel?"

"We are in a roundabout way, those people searching for us have forced me to attempt to get there another way, that's all," John was forced to admit as he kept a steady but careful crawl through the long grasses and weeds currently hiding him from the people hunting him and his alien mind guest.

"If push comes to shove, I can always swim down the dyke. It's not something I'm looking forward to having to do, but I will if I have to."

"No, John Philips, no water, we must keep to dry land wherever possible."

He heard the alien entity almost plead with him whilst ducking in and out of the clumps of grassy reeds, grasping and gripping each one in turn as they went.

"How are we doing? Any sign of them catching us up at all?" John wanted to know peering behind him without stopping to try to see whatever was going on back at the stream dyke bridge, only for almost total darkness to greet his gaze.

"I can detect that the helicopter has begun searching again. It is heading this way. Quickly wrap yourself in as much fauna as possible then curl up and lay as still as you can, John Philips."

He needed no second warning doing exactly as the alien entity told him, grabbing as much of the grassy reeds as he could hold, then huddled down in a foetal position staying as low to the dyke water as possible.

A moment later, they heard as the helicopter fly straight overhead and continued onwards following the path of the stream the danger over or so they thought.

"We made it, I don't think they saw us. We might just make it after all," brayed a jubilant John releasing the grassy cloak and sitting up on the bank peering in the direction of the distant helicopter, but the alien had other ideas.

"Do not speak too soon, John Philips, they have extremely good technology aboard that vehicle. Perhaps they have already reported their find and they are closing in on us right now," rattled off his far more sceptical mind mate as they both watched the helicopter fly back for fifty feet then stop and hover there facing the hidden child.

"No, no, they can't have. No, we can still make it," John responded matter of factly, the wide-eyed boy determined to continue onwards along the bank of the stream, only to see something to catch his peripheral vision.

"Hey, what's that over there?"

Movements in the darkness just up ahead below the hovering helicopter which were noticed simultaneously by his ever-vigilant alien ally peering out as well.

"I was right! They've found us, John Philips, they have found us!" The thunderstruck alien essence inside his head yelled as dark, shadowy shapes began appearing in the surrounding blackness; they were about to be captured by the enemy.

"Run, John Philips, run for your life, and mine. RUN!"

"Oh shit! They may be all around us but I know Hornsea better than any of them," barked back the spirited boy turning left and running as fast as he could across a small field of short wet grass hoping to outmanoeuvre those chasing him.

"That's the spirit, John Philips, run like a mountain gazelle to elude those that would do us both harm," coaxed a suddenly nervous extra-terrestrial with an enthusiastic tone of voice as its human counterpart sprinted hard in order to escape the danger homing in on them.

John knew that there were quite a few ways of exiting the field but ran in sheer panic directly across it, heading in the direction of the nearby cindered train track.

The sounds of soldiers yelling instructions behind him were soon extinguished by helicopter rotor blades but no bright lights at all as it hovered above the sprinting boy.

"They will be utilising both infrared as well as ultraviolet technology and therefore have a definite advantage over us, John Philips," advised an equally panic-stricken alien entity, suddenly fearing the worst as they had seemingly strolled headlong into a trap, a thing they needed to escape at all costs.

"Get me, er us, out of here and to my space vessel before they have the chance to do anything. Run, John Philips, run."

John did just that, sprinting as hard as the wet grass allowed, getting reasonably close to the low fence before feeling something strike him high up on the back of his left thigh.

"Aagh! Ow! Wh…what was that? Some…something hit me on the back of my leg!"

"Yes, I felt it as well. Keep moving and I will ascertain just what might have happened to us, John Philips," announced the quizzically concerned ET as a second object struck the boy's opposite thigh, this one bringing a pained yelp from a still sprinting John.

"They are firing some type of high-powered darts at you to try and stop you, presumably a tranquilliser of one kind or another. I'll try and slow its actions down, keep running."

John heard the voice tell him as his thoughts began jumbling and forcing him to stray from the direction he was heading as the fast-acting drug began to take effect.

The groggy boy made it to the waist-high fence and grabbed hold only to feel another dart smack into his left thigh; the alien in his head fighting to fend it off.

Despite every effort, all was lost as John tried desperately to climb over the fence, only for his strength to suddenly desert him altogether.

A moment later, everything went even blacker as he lost first his footing and then his consciousness, toppling helplessly over the fence to the ground below.

"John Philips? John Philips? JOHN PHILIPS!" The concerned alien entity yelled on returning to the boy's front brain lobe, only to find himself alone in there, the drug had done the business and knocked him out.

Without help from the earth boy, all was lost, mused the forlorn extra-terrestrial to itself. There had to be a way to get back to the vessel, there had to be…

"Colonel Smithlington, it's Captain Stainger here. We've got the boy complete with ET, what do you want me to do with them both; over?" The trim bearded army officer confirmed a slight smugness in his voice having succeeded in the task of locating and capturing the alien housing child.

"Excellent news, Captain, erm yes, take them to one of the empty portacabins at the Mere-side, lock them inside then post a couple of men outside just in case," informed an elated Colonel Smithlington on the other end of the line over at the town's Hall Garth Park still trying to access the reclaimed spaceship.

"Believe me, the last thing we need is for them to escape and the alien to get back to its ship. It will set us back big time and end your career in the process."

"Don't worry, Colonel, they'll be there, you have my word on it," spluttered the aggrieved army captain knowing that orders are orders and not to disobey one, even ones issued by a bona fide bastard like Colonel Smithlington.

The call ended abruptly in his ear, forcing him to relay the colonel's orders to the men under his command determined to do exactly what he knew he had to do.

The mission was accomplished now that they had the boy and alien in custody; now they were free to continue with operation 'Free Zone' protecting the flying saucer and its secrets.

Chapter Five

"John Philips? John Philips! John Philips!" The concerned alien voice deep in the mind of the groggy boy bleated as he began regaining consciousness having been knocked out a few hours earlier at the stream dyke field.

"John Philips? Speak to me, John Philips!"

"Whe…where? What? Whe…where am I?" A drowsy, disorientated John Philips groaned through an expression fogged by pain, not having a single clue as to his location only the voice urgently calling his name.

"John Philips, we appear to have been locked somewhat securely inside a room of some kind. I need to know if we are anywhere near my vessel," blurted the alien entity with more than a little panic as John lay grunting his displeasure having been deposited on a low camp bed and covered by several blankets.

"I…I couldn't tell you. Give me a second or so and I'll try to find out. Ooh, my head!" The out-of-sorts boy spluttered, blinking rapidly to help gain focus in the brightly lit room he had awoken in having spent time outside in the pitch blackness.

"Recover as quickly as you can, John Philips, then rise and take a look outside through the glass portal," boomed the slightly disgruntled alien entity now in his temporal lobe, doing nothing to aid his all-round feeling of wellbeing, nor the sudden disappointment at getting captured.

Wherever they had been taken, he couldn't know for certain but what he was able to ascertain was that he was in a portacabin, perhaps one of the ones on the Mere-side itself.

At first, he felt far too weak to move but slowly his strength returned, allowing him to climb out of the camp bed and cross the short distance to one of the two small windows.

The windows though slatted had been sealed and could not be opened by him nor seen out of they were so dirty; a quick rub with a blanket soon sorted that out.

"It…it's very dark out there but I can hear talking. I can also hear the sounds of ropes clanging against yacht masts. We're at the Mere-side alright," gushed a knowledgeable John Philips, suddenly realising that he recognised the various sounds associated with many visits to the town's freshwater lake.

"There will be guards posted out there as well no doubt, you must scour this place for a way out. Look high and low, John Philips, there has to be an escape route somewhere. Search for me so that I can get to my vessel and depart your planet," pleaded the desperately want away alien entity suddenly fearing the prospect of being imprisoned and tortured by its human hosts and exhibited like a zoo animal.

"Alright then, let's start over at the door."

On saying that, John shuffled over to the exit and tried the handle; it was unsurprisingly locked and as solid as a rock. They would not get out that way.

Turning on his heels, he caught sight of an air ventilation grill on the side wall close to the floor only to quickly discover that instead of being screwed in place it was pot riveted instead.

"Damn it, we won't be leaving through there either, but where?" The disappointed boy snorted on having bent down to inspect the grill without success, turning and staring daggers at the offending air vent.

"What about the ceiling, John Philips? The roof air ventilation unit, perhaps you can prise it open and climb through it," suggested the alien voice as the crestfallen boy gazed upwards at the ceiling overhead, seeing at once the skylight vent mentioned by the clever alien.

It was in the exact centre of the room forcing him to think of a way of getting up to it, finally deciding to use one of the chairs left behind at the computer desks to do so.

Once done, he began the ascent climbing with care and mounting exhilaration being particularly silent so as not to alert those on guard just outside the portacabin.

Thankfully for him, the tiny skylight was only partially shut but not properly sealed, instantly giving both John and the extra-terrestrial visitor rising hope of escape.

Standing on tip toes, he just managed to get a half-decent hold on the ceiling vent itself, gripping the clasp and yanking it as wide open as it could go.

"Damn it! We'll never get out through there. What now?" A furrow-browed John hissed as he gazed at the disappointingly small seven inch gap; it was far too tiny even for him to crawl his way out of.

"You can do it, John Philips, but only if you can grab hold of a thin-ended metal implements from below and then climb back up again to open it by force," voiced the seemingly unphased alien having checked out the area around the ageing skylight, seeing at once how rusted it looked to him through the Earthling's eyes.

"I mean it. There is a good chance that we can once again put our joint strengths into breaking out of this prison and getting me back to my vessel. Come on, John Philips."

John had no choice but to comply with the more knowledgeable extra-terrestrial entity's plan, gingerly climbing back down to the floor to start searching.

"The...there's nothing here, nothing we can use. What do we do now?" A bitterly disappointed John snapped having scoured the entire room, only to come up empty-handed, without an object they would not leave the building at all.

"What about your garb? Is there anything sharp and metallic on you? A belt. The buckle of your belt, remove it, John Philips."

"I don't think it's strong enough! I'll try it and see," warbled the unimpressed boy slipping his belt off and staring at the flimsy buckle with a sudden lack of enthusiasm, surely the thing was far too small.

"Reascend immediately and see what we can do. Hurry, my young human friend, and get me to my vessel, come."

John did as requested, climbing back up the table and chair ladder almost toppling over at one point but regaining his balance to complete the task in one piece.

Once back holding the skylight vent hatch, both he and the ET in his head began closely scrutinising it; the intelligent alien seeing straight away the weakness they should work on.

"There, John Philips, the metal clasp holding it in place is in increasing stress damage. If we can snap it off, you might be able to squeeze out through the opening, yes."

John acquiesced though without conviction, gripping the buckle and attacking the rusted skylight clasp with the belt spike, gentle at first, then with more and more aggression.

Slowly but surely, the spike chipped away at the rusty fastening until finally, the alien entity told him to stop and try to force it open with his bare hands.

Flopping the belt over his right shoulder, he did just that, the confident boy grabbing the air vent hatch with both hands and began snapping it backwards and forwards.

"It…it's getting loose, it's definitely about to break," hissed John through gritted teeth as the vent cover rocked to and fro on its solitary hinge, forcing his ET lodger to use his own mind to increase the youngster's strength levels.

The extra energy quickly enabled the grimacing boy to snap the vent hatch hinge off altogether, only for the thing to fly out of his hands and bang loudly on the portacabin roof.

The faint talking they could hear between the two guards down below suddenly ceased altogether forcing the alien entity into action.

"They have heard us. Quickly, John Philips, climb down, replace the chair back, and lie down on the resting place right now!" The alien voice in his head yelped, forcing John to instantly do just that, trusting the friendly extra-terrestrial implicitly. They needed each other after all.

"The very last thing we want is for them to suspect that we have located an exit point, everything must seem exactly how it should be. Now hurry."

Acting on an impulse, he reached up and quickly flipped the skylight hatch back into place before clambering on down to the floor and grabbing the chair from the table.

"Faster, John Philips, they are already at the portal," blurted his wise but annoying off-world squatter with justified urgency in its deep voice, speaking over the sound of keys rattling in the lock across from him.

He had quite literally leapt into the tiny camp bed when the door pushed open and two soldiers entered the room along with a blast of cold night air.

"Check the kid's chest, Billy, that noise might have been ET trying to break its way out of him. Be real careful now," boomed a stubble-faced second soldier both wearing infrared night-vision equipment, switching them off on entering the brightly lit portacabin.

"Shut it, Monkmon, everything seems okay in here, I think he's fast asleep. Kid? Kid? Wake up," husked the slightly nervous first soldier into the room, edging ever closer to the camp bed and the alien housing boy as if half expecting the worst.

"I said wake up, kid, or has ET eaten you alive?"

"Oom…er what did you say, Sir?" John groaned feigning being awoken from deep sleep and the drugs they shot into him hours earlier, coaxed by the devious alien in his head.

"That ought to do it. Well done, John Philips."

"Everything looks to be secure in here. Let's get back to guard duty, eh, Taylor."

"Yes, this place already gives me the creeps, come on." On saying that, the two soldiers turned and strolled back out, closing and locking the door securely behind them. John and the alien entity listened as they went.

"We have been lucky so far, John Philips, but we must still get out of here and sneak past those men before any other of your human adults arrive to seek me out."

John did not need any more incentive from his co-host springing from the camp bed and dashing across for the chair, grabbing it and placing it gingerly atop the table.

Once that was accomplished, he began climbing the combination; John taking care not to make too much noise en route on his way to the summit.

After one horrible moment when it seemed he was destined to topple noisily to the floor, he somehow miraculously regained his balance in heart-stopping fashion.

With his pulse pounding loudly in both ears, John reached the top and then gently lowered the vent cover over and onto the roof of the portacabin.

With strength he never knew he possessed but thanks to the alien aiding him, John reached up and forced his head and arms out through the skylight and onto the roof.

Remembering to keep as quiet as he could, he began a wriggling motion, hauling himself forward until he had all of his body safely out on the roof itself.

"Do not make a single sound, John Philips, we must find out where the guards are situated so as to better ascertain our getaway route, agreed?" The ever-vigilant alien entity urged, the comments giving him enough confidence to slowly climb to his feet then gently ease his way to the very edge of the roof and peer cautiously down.

From the scant light thrown out from the portacabin's slatted window, they could just make out the two men stood chatting away oblivious to him overhead.

"They are guarding the only way of exiting the room, let us slide down the back of the building and be away into the night. Let's go, John Philips."

John agreed, turning and tiptoeing his way along the top of the portacabin, aided as best he could by the alien via his optic nerve impulses.

"Do we need a diversion to draw them away so as to make a clean getaway? I could throw a rock or something into the yachts."

"No, John Philips, that will not be necessary. Silence along with opportunity will guide our path and me back to my vessel," informed the intelligent alien entity fearing the worst in the hands of human kind, wanting only to leave the third planet from the sun altogether. John had other ideas…

"What happens if they do turn up any moment now, find us gone, and start looking? They'll know exactly which way we went."

"Go on, John Philips, you arouse my curiosity?" His extra-terrestrial side kick quizzed as the Earth boy lowered himself as quietly as he could into a sitting position atop the wind-buffeted portacabin.

"We have to have something that will keep them right here even after they find us missing, and I have just the thing."

"Aargh yes, releasing a waterborne vessel so as to assume that we are aboard, yes."

"I thought that you weren't going to do that to me? Anyhow yes, that is what I mean," growled a miffed John annoyed that his alien mind guest was once again reading his thoughts and saying them out loud; something he did not particularly enjoy it doing.

"Apology proffered, John Philips, but can you do it without the guards seeing you with their night-vision equipment?" The agreeable extra-terrestrial asked with all sincerity, actually liking the idea in principle if the truth be known. John lowered himself over the edge and dropped to the grass below.

"I should be able to. There's always the possibility that they might see me but surely it's worth doing just to get us time to get to your spaceship, isn't it? It won't take very long."

With that, he began edging his way along the back of the line of newly erected portacabins and from there, around the main building well out of sight of the two guards.

Once he had circumnavigated the Mere-side cafe building, he peered to his left in the general direction of the portacabins, seeing a tiny speck of light and the chatting guards standing there.

Taking a deep breath, John began a low lopping run across the short grass pathway and out onto the last one of four wooden wave-splashed jetties and laid down on it.

After a full minute, it was obvious that he had not been noticed by either of the two guards so it was safe to continue, using each of the water-soaked slats to haul himself along by.

After five long minutes of pulling, sliding, and stopping to check on the guards, he finally made it to the end of the wooden jetty undetected and lay listening in the darkness.

When he was quite sure that they had not seen or heard him at all, John began untying the very last row boat of the double ranks bobbing noisily on either side of him.

Once untied, he turned the empty boat around, whilst forcing it outwards towards the centre of the enormous freshwater lake's vast expanse of choppy water.

Without waiting at all, he turned and began the return journey, crawling back using the same method as before, reaching the path only for flashing lights to catch his eye.

"They have arrived, John Philips. May I suggest that we 'high tail it' away from here as fast as you can run, agreed," barked his insecure alien mind tenant lodged deep inside John's buzzing brain, becoming instantly alerted to the danger they both found themselves in.

With speed he didn't know he possessed, John sprinted hard for the main building knowing as he did that all eyes would be on the vehicles approaching the Mere-view peninsula.

Once undercover and spurred on by the equally nervous alien, he kept running, passing the crazy golf and down a slight incline, then turned right, stumbling occasionally as he went.

Luckily for him, his path led him just wide of the geese nesting area but close enough to wake and disturb one or two; his plan seemed to be working after all.

"How are our troublesome 'friends' getting on, Corporal?" A smiling Colonel Smithlington smarmed having climbed from the staff car and straightened his tunic, receiving a crisp salute as expected from all subordinate ranks.

"Have either of them been a nuisance at all, I trust not?"

"As good as gold, Sir, no trouble," responded the bearded soldier as he and his colleague stood to attention in front of the row of portacabins, the middle one, in particular, seeing it held the young alien housing boy.

"Good. Now unlock the door, then lock it again once we are inside just to be on the safe side," ordered the business-like colonel flanked as he was by another senior high-ranking officer and an unsmiling dark-suited civilian, both eager to engage the human alien anomaly inside.

"Right, you are, Sir."

On saying that, the blank-faced corporal turned and walked the short distance to the portacabin door along with his fellow guard, the key already held out ready to use.

Without hesitating, he inserted the key, unlocked the door, and then held it open for the newly arrived trio to enter, all three striding past him into the building.

"Corporal! Corporal! Get in here, the boy! He! He's not here! They've gone!" A mortified Colonel Smithlington shrieked at the top of his voice, instantly bringing the two soldiers running into the building as the full implications of the loss hit home.

"Whe…where are they? Up there, look. He must have somehow prised open the roof vent hatch and gotten out onto the top of the portacabin," commented the stoney expressioned civilian pointing a thin digit upwards in the direction of the wide open ventilation hatch; all five men staring at the offending ceiling vent.

"Didn't either of you two clowns hear or see anything?" A crimson Colonel Smithlington snarled turning to face the pair of worried-looking soldiers staring helplessly back having failed to do the simple task assigned to them.

"Actually, th…there was quite a loud noise from in here but on investigation, we found the boy on the camp bed; apart from that, not a peep, Sir," admitted the red-faced corporal rubbing at his dark beard as the three angry-looking high-ranking visitors stared back in complete bewilderment and incrimination.

"We'll deal with the court martials later. Well, Corporal, any idea as to where they could have gone, have you?" A furrow-browed Colonel Smithlington asked, his expression a mask of undisguised disappointment, his only hope was that one of them could now save the day.

"Don't fret on, Sir, we've got an infrared advantage over him. If he's out there, we will soon find him. Come on, Phil, erm, I mean Corporal Partridge," proffered a suddenly animated Corporal Taylor, a nervous twitch clearly noticeable on his bearded left cheek as both he and fellow under fire colleague, Partridge, exited the building.

By the time both men were outside, they had deftly pulled down and flicked on their infrared night-vision scopes, each soldier walking slowly outwards in different directions.

"Nothing so far, Sir, hang on a mo…what's that? Colonel, there is a row boat out in the middle of the lake," blurted a quizzical Corporal Taylor having reached and strode on to and along one of the row boat tethered wooden jetty, seeing almost immediately the vessel out on the choppy lake.

"It definitely shouldn't be out there, it ought to be tied up against the jetty with all of the others. What do you think, Sir?"

"There's only one thing for it, you lost hint so you and your bungling colleague can row out there and bring him back," grunted their unsmiling superior officer, his words interrupted momentarily by the sound of honking geese making him and his two guests turn and peer into the darkness behind them.

"Did you order me and Corporal Partridge to go out there this time of night, Sir?"

"Yes, Corporal, I am ordering you two to jump into a boat and get going; right now, soldier," snapped back the unphased colonel knowing that he was determined to do whatever it took to get the alien-bearing boy back and punish his lackadaisical men en route.

"Colonel Smithlington, is there any way that we can watch what is going on out there on the water at all?"

"Why, yes, there is Professor Pendlewith. We should be able to see events unfold via the infrared camera apparatus affixed to both night-vision helmets. Come on, gents, this way."

With that, Colonel Smithlington led his two colleagues back and into the staff car, closing the doors behind them as the corporals untied a boat and began rowing.

By utilising the soldiers' infrared helmet attachment antennas and switching to a pre-selected channel, the trio were able to suddenly see what the two rowers were seeing.

The chasing row boat was now well underway and cutting through the windswept waters of Hornsea Mere some fifty metres behind the fleeing vessel bobbing up and down ahead of them.

"Still no sign of him yet, Colonel. My guess is that he's hiding at the bottom of the boat hoping that we haven't seen it out on the lake," grunted the bearded soldier of the pair sent to retrieve the boy along with the alien entity he was purported to be housing though he was not to reason why.

They were now barely twenty metres away from the boat bouncing rhythmically on the choppy waters clearly visible in the pale green illuminated night light.

"Just a few more pulls and we'll have the little runaway. Come on, Phil, heave, a bit further," husked a breathless Corporal Taylor as they drew ever closer to the target vessel and its elusive occupant. A moment later, they pulled alongside and peered into it.

"Hey, it…it's empty! He…he's not here. Where the hell has he gone?"

"We can see that, you idiot. Check it over anyway just in case he's hiding. What about the lake itself?" A seemingly unphased Colonel Smithlington responded via the two-way communications device connecting them; shock registering in the corporal's voice as he answered his superior officer.

"Colonel, there is a 'no swimming, water's dangerous' sign back at the boat house. Apparently, there are leg tangling reeds not to mention lots of pike, the freshwater shark, in it," gushed the knowledgeable corporal having read up on the seaside resort, discovering that it was home to Hornsea Mere, the biggest freshwater lake in all of Yorkshire.

"Surely even a local boy like him wouldn't dare to ignore such well-warned dangers. I know that I wouldn't do it if I were him. Besides, he'd be easy to see out there."

"Very well, point taken. Get yourselves back here and bring the other boat as well. We will just have to admit that the boy has gone and outfoxed us, that's all," drawled a clearly miffed Colonel Smithlington, rubbing a dry palm over the top of his bald pate, something he tended to do when in certain tense situations.

"I'll get the helicopter back in. They will soon locate him. He, or they, will be making for the Hall Garth Park and the alien ship, that's where we are heading."

A moment later, the transmission ended leaving the two corporals to row back to shore as Professor Pendlewith suddenly found his voice.

"Colonel Smithlington, I suggest that you order your men to do the right thing and completely surround the park and its many entrances and exits."

"The professor is right you know. He, or rather 'they', will definitely be going for the alien spacecraft so that is what we have got to deny it and defend," agreed the high-ranking officer sat immediately behind the other two men; he being there simply to observe the smooth running of what was an extremely important operation.

"That's what I fully intend to do once I have ordered the helicopter back. We'll soon have that park locked down tighter than America's 'Area 52'. Excuse me, gentlemen."

Once Colonel Smithlington had finished making the calls, they headed for the town's Hall Garth Park determined to keep their highly prized asset whatever the cost.

Once passed the hostile, hissing geese, it was reasonably easy to locate and then edge his way around the very end fence post and into the next field along.

His clever ruse back at the Mere-side should hopefully keep them busy and distracted enough for him to flee the area and reach the park and then on to the spaceship.

Unfortunately for him, the next field along turned out to be a nightmare of thick, boggy reed beds and ankle-deep lake water; all impossible to avoid in the darkness.

He had wandered into an area on the very edge of the freshwater lake left deliberately that way to entice wildlife to build a home and nest there free from danger and disturbance.

If memory served right, it was only a short distance to the dry land, houses, and children's play area, but to John, it seemed to be far longer and fraught with danger at every turn.

It was a veritable minefield in the utter darkness as unexpected ankle-deep water followed sprawling falls, all the while warned by the alien to be silent or risk discovery.

Finally, following quite a freezing cold, sometimes painful journey, he found himself stumbling into a slatted wooden fence; he'd reached the other side.

"We appear to have made that particular journey but we have no time to stand resting, John Philips, we must exit this area and get closer to my vessel," droned the irritating alien entity inside his head, angering the cold, wet, tired boy in the process. John wanted only to go home and fall fast asleep but knew he couldn't do that.

"Y…yes, let's…let's get going. There's an alley that runs up into the centre of town between a couple of houses and shops, it'll bring us out quite close to the park and your spaceship," volunteered the knowledgeable boy, beginning a brisk walk in the direction he knew the thin narrow passageway could be found; it linked the Mere-side with the town centre.

Locating the alley wasn't easy but after a couple of clumsy and almost embarrassing attempts, he found it, walking to within four steps of the main road when a familiar sound made him stop and turn.

"It is the search helicopter, they have called it in. Soon the whole town will be crawling with soldiers. We have got to get into the park right now, John Philips, it's our last chance," yelped the distinctly panic-stricken alien entity suddenly flitting between hemispheres of his brain such was its agitated state at the thought of being captured.

"Don't worry, we are only a stone's throw from the park, it's just behind that church over there."

On saying that, John continued walking to the very end and took a quick look around. All was dark, windswept, and silent as the grave; it was going to be easy, too easy.

Breaking into a run, John began a diagonal dash towards the unlit parish church, getting half way across when everything took a massive turn for the worst.

Suddenly, the silent, frightening claustrophobic blackness of his surroundings began sparking and flashing as land rovers approached from all three directions at once.

Instead of spurring him on, it seemed to have the complete opposite effect, slowing the strangely mesmerised boy like a rabbit caught in a car's main beam headlights.

To the shock and horror of his alien counterpart, John slowed to a halt and stood looking around him at the search vehicles as their head lamps and spotlights rounded the bends simultaneously.

"Run, John Philips, run! Snap out of it and RUN!" The distraught alien barked, bouncing aggressively to try and get his full attention, which it quickly managed to do, John snapped out of it and set off in a sprint.

With scant seconds remaining and the entire area around him now as light as day thanks to the powerful spotlights mounted on the trio of arriving vehicles, he reached the other side.

Using one of the two long wooden benches, he jumped up onto it and launched himself over the high stone wall, landing painfully in the graveyard beyond.

"Remain as still as you possibly can, John Philips, or they may discover where we are hidden," hissed his extra-terrestrial temporary soulmate with conviction, speaking low even though they were both inside the head of the human boy and only they could hear it.

"We could do with seeing exactly where they all are and what is going on, well, John Philips?"

"Erm, ther…there's a big crack in the wall along by the other wooden park bench. If there isn't anything blocking it off, I may be able to see them without them seeing me."

That's what he did, crawling and wriggling like a snake along the foot of the church wall itself until he reached what was quite a noticeable crack with light pouring in through it.

Once settled and comfortable, John peered out through the crack in the wall, noting straight away that the three vehicles were parked bumper to bumper and their crews talking animatedly.

"I can only surmise that they are discussing their briefs and in which order they will be circling the park," explained the more experienced and knowledgeable alien entity as it utilised the boy's visionary senses to see for itself exactly where they both stood in the current circumstances.

"Once they begin to do just that, it will leave us free to go and fulfil our task, John Philips. Let us start easing ourselves away from the danger of discovery and capture this place still holds for us both."

John did just that, turning on hands and knees then beginning a slow waddling motion gripping and easing himself around each icy cold headstone in turn as he went.

It was slow going but he could not afford to make any noise whatsoever, not if they were to remain one step ahead of the men trying to stop them.

Utilising the bright light from the trio of land rovers, he was able to actually see a little of the terrain around him, making it to the parish church just as the three vehicles pulled apart.

"They are leaving, we've done it. Hey, what is that sound?" A momentarily jubilant John hissed, only for the oh-so-familiar noise of distant rotor blades growing steadily closer to furrow his brow with sudden worry.

"It is the helicopter. We need to get into hiding, John Philips, there is not a moment to lose!" The panic-stricken alien volunteered, half of the equation as the three land rovers began driving away each in a different direction from the others.

"SHIT! The tomb! There's an empty grave! Me and my friends discovered it by accident. If it's still there that is; now which one is it?" The lightheaded boy responded whilst desperately attempting to get his exact bearings in the cramped, rapidly darkening, church graveyard as the helicopter grew ominously closer.

"Erm, yes there, that one over there."

John was already up on his feet and in a crouched run heading for what he hoped was the long empty sarcophagus-style grave at the far end of the row before him.

"Hurry, John Philips, they are almost upon us," squawked his worried alien mind guest as the search flight from the approaching helicopter began flickering over the shops and buildings, arriving any moment now.

With dogged determination, John quickly reached the grave they were both desperate to hide in but not before bashing knee-first into the upright stone immediately ahead of it.

On limping up to the horizontal grave, he recalled the method he and his pals used to enter and exit the claustrophobic confines when playing 'raising the dead' together.

They had devised a speedy method of gripping and then sliding the very left edge of the concrete slab so that it swivelled enough to allow a young child to climb inside.

That was exactly what he did, sliding hurriedly into it, only to find that it had been filled with assorted grave-digging things, making it difficult but not impossible to fit inside.

With the helicopter flying over the church and graveyard, John put his strength and know-how into resealing the concrete lid, managing it on the third time of asking.

"Do you think they saw us at all?" A close to exhausted John Philips panted as he lay uncomfortably atop not only grave-digging equipment but also drums of strong smelling weed killer as well.

"Only time will tell, as you Earth dwellers say. We will wait a few of your minutes then take a look outside," purred back the somehow reassuring alien entity in the freezing cold sarcophagus; the remark doing nothing to alter the sneer of displeasure fixed on John's face thanks to the smell.

"Damn, it stinks in here. Have we had two minutes yet?" A gurning John wanted to know; the smell getting stronger and more concentrated the longer the concrete slab remained in place sealing him inside.

"Try to stay calm for just a few more of your Earth seconds, my young friend, panic will achieve nothing."

The extra-terrestrial was right, annoyingly so, mused John. The shivering boy wanted only to throw open the slab and leap out of the stinking concrete coffin but knew better.

He could only grin and bear it as the air began to get sparse inside his necessary incarceration, then his off-worldly co-host gave him the news he was waiting for.

"Alright, John Philips, you can push open the lid but not too far, we should quickly notice them if they are still anywhere in the area."

A relieved John did just that, utilising the same method he and his friends used to do, pushing his right shoulder up and sideway sliding it open several inches then stopping.

"We have been somewhat successful, John Philips, they are still close by but it is safe to continue; let us go."

John was only too pleased to escape the claustrophobic confines. The raggedy breathing boy forced the heavy lid wide open and leapt out, returning it into position in the dark graveyard.

"They will soon return, we must leave this area at once if we are to get to my vessel, John Philips," urged the wantaway alien entity, almost sensing how near they were to his vessel and an escape from the third planet back out into the depths of the multiverses.

"We are almost there. I'll just make my way around the church and over the wall into the park itself, we'll soon get to your flying saucer."

On saying that, John began making his way between the minefield of barely visible grave stones, managing to bump into nearly all of them en route back to the main pathway.

Once on the path touching the 'house of God' local branch, it was quite a lot easier and less painful as the extreme lack of any light whatsoever made each footstep potentially dangerous.

With one hand touching the stone walls to save bumping into any more gravestones, John edged his way around the building egged on by the talkative alien.

It was impossibly dark with no light hitting his retinas and if it wasn't for the alien aiding his sense of sight and direction as best it could, he might easily get badly injured.

Everything was alright until John rounded the silhouetted house of God and remembered that the only way down to the lower grassy church hall gardens was a long narrow stone slope somewhere ahead in the blackness.

The alternative to the slope was a four foot sheer drop to the ground below, something both John and the alien entity did not want to have happen for both their sakes.

With one foot tapping out ahead of him, he found the slope and began slowly edging his way downwards; the two conjoined minds in a celebratory mood the further they went.

A moment later, they came unstuck as John's left foot slipped off the side of the ramp and he tumbled over to land in a heap on a thankfully soft, short-cut grass lawn.

As John lay groaning and rubbing his right shoulder, he was suddenly caught in the brilliant glare of a spotlight beam as one of the land rovers went passed on the main road.

"The…they saw us! What are we going to do now?" A wide-eyed John groaned sitting suddenly bolt upright on the glass as the land rover went by, slowing all the while in order to come and investigate the possible sighting.

"Quick, John Philips, they will be returning any moment now, we cannot let ourselves be caught so close to our goal."

With ET's words fresh in his own thought centre, John scrambled to his feet and turned on his heels, breaking into a fast sprint aided slightly by the red tail lights of the reversing vehicle.

Without looking back, the running boy reached the high stone wall leaping upwards and grasping the rounded concrete top whilst doing a mid-air straddle with both legs in the process.

His luck was in as John felt his feet scrape onto then slip over the top, the forward momentum forcing the rest of his body to do likewise and just in time.

Unluckily for John, he was nowhere near the gnarled S-shaped tree and its horizontal ledge, instead falling through the air at the same moment that the courtyard was flooded by the spotlight.

His fall was partly broken by a thick tangle of bramble bushes he struck on the way down, bouncing him off and launching boy and alien outwards to land painfully on the soft grass beyond.

After rolling to a halt, he quickly felt for any injuries only for the alien entity coexisting in his mind to be more concerned with their not being caught out in the open.

"Run, John Philips, they may have seen us; run for your life, for both our lives, run!"

John didn't need telling twice, climbing from the ground and, on a sudden whim, turning left and running in the opposite direction to the alien's spaceship and into the nearest copse of trees.

The young local boy chose that particular place due to it being set around a twelve feet deep gulley that was once a moat long ago when the resort had a castle and keep.

He also knew that the powerfully bright spotlight now aimed at the park itself was bound to attract unwanted attention to that area of the well-guarded Hall Garth Park.

Light from the super trooper on the other side of the high wall allowed John just enough scope to get his actual bearings as he sprinted behind the first huge tree and stood panting for breath.

"I think we are in luck, my Earth child friend. I detect no one peering over that wall for us. We have made it so far and are now very close to my vessel," crooned his off-worldly mind companion as they stood in the dark park now barely a few hundred metres from their much sought-after and well-guarded spaceship.

"But what we cannot afford to do is be too complacent and walk into a trap. I believe it is exactly what they will expect us to do."

"If they don't know that we are actually in the park, then we still have a chance. There's a low-lying area over to our left, it'll allow us to approach your vessel from behind; they might not expect that," proffered an eager John Philips, the young boy recalling the topography of the park even though it was far too dark to actually see hardly anything at all.

"Well done, John Philips, you are a quick learner. It may well get me to my vessel and you back to being yourself again. Let's get moving, shall we?"

Without replying, John turned and began making his way down the steep-sided, waist-high hill of tangled weeds and grasses, not to mention thistles and stinging nettles.

Halfway down, he felt his feet slip from under him, making John fall backwards, doing the rest of the short journey horizontally, crashing through the dense undergrowth to a sudden halt.

Groaning and cussing in the near pitch blackness, the grimacing boy clambered slowly back up again much to the amusement of the tut-tutting alien parked deep in his flustered mind.

"Anything hurt, John Philips, apart from your pride, my angry young Earthling? Come, let us get going."

John complied with the sarcastic extra-terrestrial, its comment not enjoyed by the thistle-scratched boy, pushing and forcing his way through the tangled mass ahead of him.

A minute or so later, he managed to exit the unforgiving foliage and was about to stroll onto the muddy pathway when the alien in his head with him stopped him in his tracks.

"Wait, do not walk over the very centre of the pathway in case they have placed motion-detecting devices at every entrance and exit to this park of yours, John Philips," enthused the ultra-cautious extra-terrestrial lodged in the local boy's brain, thinking like a human adult and wondering what he would do in their shoes.

"Tell me, is there another way of circumnavigating our way to my vessel apart from the land?"

"The only way I can think of is for me to climb a tree at this side and cross over to the one across from it; that's all I can suggest," admitted John, having climbed just about all of the surrounding trees at one time or another but never at night, and especially not without being able to see anything at all.

"That is what we need to do. When you are ready to go aloft and avoid the motion-detecting apparatus, you may do so, John Philips," informed a not very confident-sounding visiting alien entity as it peered up at the pitch black branches of the trees around them and the incredible dangers therein.

"Alright, this one over here, I've climbed it more than any other tree around here, though not in the dark. Still, as we say on Earth, 'there is always a first time for everything'," admitted the reluctant boy. John hesitated at first at the foot of the tree he knew to be a horse chestnut, having climbed it lots of times searching for the so far illusive giant 'super conker' but never came across one.

Knowing that there was no alternative, John peered upwards trying to picture the last time he actually climbed that particular tree and what branches would give the best hand holds.

His first attempt never really got off the ground; John missed his hand hold and he stumbled back down to the ground again. Then, he started up a second time.

The next ascent proved more successful with John climbing for what seemed ages, finding it difficult, painfully so at times as a scratched face and bruised knee testified.

A few minutes and several close calls later, he was high enough to risk one or two short hand hidden bursts of light from his tiny pencil torch.

"Be careful, John Philips, light can be seen from quite a long distance at night, aim it well but don't let it be seen," warned a wary experienced other worldly alien entity fearing the worst as his human host balanced precariously halfway up a tree in an extremely dark park trying to get back home.

"Don't worry, no one will see it but you and me. I just need to find out exactly where I am, that's all," John replied as he lay flat on his stomach desperately attempting to get his right hand into his trouser pocket, finally doing so, pulling out his pencil torch in the process.

A moment later, both his cupped hands and a small area immediately around him became faintly visible, affording John and the alien entity a momentary glimpse of their position and way forward.

"Do it again, John Philips, just once more," urged his cranial co-inhabitor, to which John duly did, doing the exact same thing as a few seconds earlier, achieving almost the same result except for one thing.

"From the look of things, we have arrived at the apex of our ascent, John Philips, we can begin heading horizontally. Let's get going, my vessel is calling my name."

With those words furrowing his brow and the cool breeze tugging and tousling at his hair and clothing, John started crawling along the thick strong branch into the darkness.

With only blackness ahead of him, he adopted a breast stroke style movement as used by swimmers in order to feel for any branches in front that might hurt or knock him off altogether.

"Keep going, John Philips, we are about to establish contact with the next deciduous flora giant. We may require another very brief glow from that torch of yours."

He was busy feeling for the thin torch which he had slid back into his trouser pocket when they heard a noise, one they both knew meant trouble big time; it was the helicopter.

Chapter Six

"Listen up, you lot, there has been a report of a possibly but not definite sighting of the boy and our VIP visitor at the back of the parish church hall two minutes ago," barked an unsmiling Colonel Smithlington, having just been informed of the good news himself and was anxious to redeploy his troops into the park itself.

"I want a dozen men to make a complete sweep of that park with infrared vision straight away. I have already ordered a chopper to utilise its body heat-seeking equipment to do likewise."

"Yes, Sir, I'll get right onto it, Colonel," responded an equally professional Sergeant Broadpierce from one of the continually circling land rovers, the non-commissioned army officer already signalling for the vehicle to stop.

"I don't need to tell you how important this is to everyone in the loop, Sergeant. Get me that boy and the ET guesting in his brain or your next posting will be Antarctica counting penguins all by yourself."

On saying that, the call ended, leaving an angry Sergeant Broadpierce to take it out on the soldiers under his immediate command as instructed by his superior officer.

Back at the makeshift hanger in the town's Hall Garth Park, the unflappable Colonel Smithlington turned his attention to the still tightly sealed flying saucer.

"Are we any closer to getting that thing open, Thomkinsby?"

"Not yet, Colonel. It seems to be made of a non-metallic substance, spongy yet incredibly strong. It's resisting everything we are throwing at it up to now that is," retorted the man in charge of finding a way inside the scientific find of a lifetime as far as humanity was concerned only for it to stubbornly refuse to offer up its vast array of secrets.

"It's as we expected, the alien is using the boy to get back to its spaceship. If that happens, we stand to lose all of the vast knowledge our downed ET visitor could give us."

"That's quite right, Colonel, but surely you don't think that the boy can actually make it to the vessel, do you?" The curious army boffin quizzed, who was there to find a way into the off-worldly flying saucer dredged from the depths of the freshwater lake a couple of days ago.

"We cannot let that happen then, can we? No, we have to lure them into a sense of false security, make them think that they are about to succeed, then spring the trap," informed the officer in overall charge of engineering a way into the newly claimed alien spacecraft.

"What if they actually do make it to it, despite all of your elaborately made plans and takes off into space? What then?"

"Don't worry, we'll soon have both alien and its technology in our possession; just wait and see."

Both John and his alien other half knew full well that they were very much out in the open with absolutely nowhere to hide as far as the heat-seeking helicopter was concerned.

"Ther…there's nothing to stop them finding us, nowhere to hide; they'll find us now for certain."

"There has to be. Think, John Philips, think hard. We must make it to my vessel," urged an equally unsettled alien entity hoping that the so far clever, resourceful human boy could conjure up one more way of outsmarting his own adult kind.

"I…I…er, there was something actor Arnold Schwarzenegger did it in a movie once. It might work for us if I can manage to do it without falling off and killing myself."

On saying that, John began to slowly ease himself sideways whilst clinging on to the thick branch beneath him, desperately feeling for the one below belonging to the next tree along.

The approaching helicopter sent shock waves through both the boy and the alien entity as it hovered somewhere close by, possibly even directly overhead watching their every move.

"I see your thinking, John Philips, fully utilise the two branches so as to hopefully blot out your body heat from above," voiced the impressed extra-terrestrial as the clever, inventive boy slid even further around the upper branch, frantically feeling for and finding the one he needed.

"Just a little bit more and we might be out of danger; keep a tight hold of it, we don't want to fall."

"I…I was thinking along those lines myself. As it happens, it's a long way down, I might not survive it if I do slip off," responded the rapidly tiring boy through tightly gritted teeth as his puny muscles gave their all to help emulate a movie scene but finding it agonisingly difficult instead.

Moments later, he shuffled to a halt and lay puffing and panting for breath sandwiched between the two overlapping branches as a helicopter flew overhead.

"Well done, John Philips, I think that we may well have succeeded in our planned subterfuge. They are moving away from this area of your parkland. Let us be on our way," husked a relieved alien entity as the helicopter's rotor blades got further away with its heat-seeking device; it was time to continue towards the well-protected spaceship.

No sooner had he begun wriggling forward than he felt himself sliding sideways, slipping despite all attempts to remain there, gasping and groaning with the sheer effort involved.

"Fight the pull of your planet's gravity, John Philips, we must remain aloft or they will capture us, fight it!" The annoyingly accurate extra-terrestrial droned proffering advice that was both extremely obvious and irritatingly distracting at the same time as he battled to keep on the branch.

For a nerve-jangling moment, he almost lost his grip altogether, only to regain the hold but not the strength to haul himself back up again, the alternative was to fall.

"Hold on, John Philips, I will try to stimulate your muscular and inner strength centres, that should help to expel the build-up of lactic acid that is making you tired."

True to its word, the alien entity did just that, flitting over to that area of his mind and setting things in motion allowing him to clamber back up onto the branch.

"I knew you could do it, John Philips, if we put our minds to it. Let's be on our way, shall we?"

John heard the alien drone as he lay panting for breath atop the thick branch in the pitch blackness directly beneath the larger one overhead.

"We make a good team on this third planet of yours, John Philips, but I still look forward to blasting off into space though," said his restless ET colleague trying to press the fearless Earth child to continue onwards, so desperate was the other worldly entity to reach its spaceship and depart.

"Y…yes, alright. I need to go straight ahead for three of my own body lengths, then begin climbing upwards."

On saying that, John started a slow crawl along the sturdy branch, feeling his way along like a blind person, being doubly careful not to fall or injure himself at all.

"Th…this should be about right. There's a long series of zig-zagged branches, I can use them like steps to haul myself along with; me and my gang built them last year," revealed John whilst peering up into the all but hidden treetops, knowing full well the way he had to go but also the dangers and difficulties involved as well.

"Stop moving and remain perfectly still, John Philips, we have unwanted company. Soldiers are currently all around us in the park seeking to find us using infrared equipment," hissed the knowledgeable alien in his head having used John's senses to get a better idea of what was going on whilst the young boy continued climbing the tree.

"I suggest that you stretch out along this branch and do not move a single muscle. I will tell you when is safe for us to continue onwards."

John did just that, stopping and doing exactly what the alien suggested, laying as still as possible amidst the creaking, windswept branches all around him.

Voices! He could hear the sound of men talking somewhere in the darkness down below; not what they were saying, only the odd word and bursts of static from their devices.

John lay there silently listening, only just hearing them over the sound of the wind rustling through the leafy branches around both him and the concentrating alien in his head.

The resourceful alien had been proved correct in that; a massive search of the park was currently underway in an all-out attempt to discover their whereabouts.

All John could do was to remain as still as he possibly could and wait it out, after all, how could they know where they were? No, they were only guessing.

Again, the sound of rotor blades informed them that they were being revisited by the search helicopter; John worried but the alien entity was not ruffled at all.

"Remain perfectly still, John Philips, otherwise we will be an even easier target than we are now. Aahh, good! The humans down on the ground have turned and are reversing the search."

John heard the alien utter in response to his fear and uncertainty as to the outcome of their nocturnal journey and keeping his word to get them to the spaceship.

"We have to get to my vessel so that I can evacuate this mind of yours and return to my own, only then will I be able to escape this treacherous planet and back to the relative safety of the stars."

"Whe…where will you go once you finally leave Earth?"

John wanted to know; his question seemed to catch the unphasable alien entity out having not expected him to ask such a thing nor indeed be able to understand the answer.

"I am uncertain as to my next destination, John Philips, I might go back to my own home world, or relax on Kraxxoss moon 379, I'm not sure," droned his wantaway mind guest, its indecisiveness strangely reassuring to the young boy shivering with cold and dampness halfway up a sycamore tree in the dead of night.

"Kraxxoss moon 379, sounds interesting. Where about is it from here? I might know it. We did astronomy this term at school."

"Very well, John Philips, head straight for Brrooaaeekka…er or what you know it as 'Pliaddes', from there…"

"Pliaddes! The 'seven sisters'!" The knowledgeable boy exclaimed having recognised the constellation. straight away and couldn't help but let his super intelligent ET know that he did so.

"As I was telling you, John Philips, once through the vastness of Brrooaaeekka, it's another nine hundreds of your 'light years', then slingshot around the star Msshaannreeilp towards Kraxxoss."

"I'm glad I asked," groaned a nonplussed John, his mind unable to comprehend such incredibly vast distances; his comment noted by the alien entity still concentrating on events on the ground down below.

"Good news, John Philips, the men on the ground have proceeded far enough along for us to continue our progress towards my own vessel and much-anticipated departure from your world."

It was music to John's icy cold ears, such was his desperation to get going as well, especially now that the wind had gotten up and was threatening to dislodge him at any moment.

With safety in mind, the furrow-browed boy began a slow crawl along the solid branch, reaching the trunk, then standing up and making his way around it to the other side.

Once John had successfully semi-circumnavigated the tree trunk, he started climbing upwards, only two branches before beginning a perilously dangerous shuffle along the wind-whipped tightrope.

It was slow going as the trees responded to the freshening wind now gusting into him through the park, making progress difficult but not impossible for John and the wantaway alien.

The next tree along provided a much stiffer challenge as most of the upper branches were a lot thinner than they needed to be to support his weight.

"Oh no! Whooa there! Damn! I almost fell just then. I know, I went up when I should have climbed downwards."

"Do not let that happen, John Philips. If you die, I will not be able to get to my vessel, I do not want it to end here either," volunteered the equally on edge alien entity in response to his young host's troubled admission, its only concern being to get to its vessel whatever the cost.

John instantly began climbing downwards desperately attempting to remember exactly which branch was where having spent many a long afternoons going from tree to tree, branches to branches, in daylight but never at night.

Five minutes and several near calamitous falls later, he stood somewhat triumphantly on the branch he had originally sought in the first instance, only something wasn't quite right.

Suddenly, and without warning, the branch he was standing on snapped, disappearing underfoot and sending him plunging forward and down, thudding into the branch below.

Despite yells of encouragement from his alien mind guest, John was knocked out cold, falling to the ground unconscious amidst a pile of leaves and wet grass, dead to the world…

"Nothing? Nothing at all? Not a single sign of him anywhere! I find that very hard to believe, especially with the technology we have at our disposal," quizzed a perplexed disbelieving Colonel Smithlington, noting the anguished nod from his subordinate officer whose men had scoured the entire park and surrounding area with no success.

"May I suggest that you and your unit go back and do it again, Mister, this time send a team down to the Mere-side to work their way to the park, we know where they are heading."

"Do you authorise us to enter any shops and buildings if they are unlocked and we deem it necessary, Sir?"

The captain wanted to know, the seasoned soldier hoping that his stickler superior officer had changed his mind about prohibiting anyone from entering buildings without strict authority.

"Certainly not, only garages, greenhouses, sheds and outside privies, got that, Captain. Now go and get me that boy and that's an order."

On saying that, Colonel Smithlington ended the conversation, watching unsmilingly at his disgruntled subordinate colleague turned and exited the makeshift hanger bristling with rage.

"How close are we to opening that spaceship?" The under-pressure colonel asked, having been given the official task of finding out what lay within the flying disc, something he was determined to do whatever the cost.

"We are very close to discovering its power source but we will still need its pilot to get us inside it."

"Don't worry, Thomkinsby, you'll get our alien visitor quite soon now; once here, we will all get to see the inside of its spaceship and a lot more besides," volunteered the confident-sounding colonel rubbing both big hands together as he did so, his fellow army colleague remaining unsure as to the final end result in all this.

"That twelve year old local kid sure knows his way around this town, wouldn't you say, Colonel? He seems to have managed to run rings around those highly trained troops of yours."

Technician Thomkinsby's comments would normally have earned him a savage rebuke by the officer in command, only for it to be all but ignored by a smirking Colonel Smithlington.

"Yes, the child certainly does know this town like the back of his hand, but sooner or later, he'll come unstuck and then we will have the pair of them, you'll see, my son," The colonel drawled back at him his voice low and authoritative, giving the distinct and deliberate impression that nothing could, or would, possibly go wrong with his plans.

"Anyway, shouldn't you be over there trying to find a way to get that saucer's doors open? Well, snap to it then, Mister."

Colonel Smithlington sat watching the technician stride away in the direction of the makeshift hanger and the priceless object within.

"Colonel, it's the chopper, they've found something in the park. Apparently, it's the right size and shape to be our target," announced his suddenly animated communications officer, turning as if stung by a wasp in her eagerness to relay the message to the waiting military man.

"Excellent news! At last, we've got him! Radio the captain and give him the coordinates from the helicopter, then tell the pilot not to let the boy out of his sight until they get there, that's all."

Whilst his orders were being relayed, the smiling colonel leaned back in his chair, clapping both hands noisily together in his customary act of personal victory.

If their luck held steady, they would soon have the alien-hosting boy under secure and inescapable confinement. From there, the rest would be easy.

This time, there would be no mistakes. The errant alien's spaceship and secrets therein would be his for the taking, then passed over to his government for closer scrutiny.

Two minutes later, came the call he'd been waiting anxiously to receive; the boy and alien had been found, where did he want him taken?

"Tell him to take them to the mobile operations vehicle parked at the main entrance to the park and I'll meet them there once I finish up here," volunteered the beaming officer-in-charge of overall recovery and retrieval of all things associated with both the alien and the technical information it possessed.

"Cover the boy's eyes and ears en route just in case our ET friend decides to leave us. Do not lose them again, we need that alien or we'll all get posted to Antarctica."

With the message well and truly delivered, Colonel Smithlington clapped his huge hands against one another in utter triumph as the communications officer looked across at him, both knowing that they were about to succeed at long last.

"We are about to make history, Perkins, the first human beings to talk to a bona fide extra-terrestrial; that's if the top brass don't get here first."

"Can I speak off the record, Colonel, man to man? It might be important." The woman sat at the communication console asked, staring at her superior officer, a thought running through her mind; one that she couldn't shake off no matter how hard she tried.

"Go ahead, Perkins, what's on your mind?"

"I guess we've all seen all of those angry attacking alien warships trying to wipe out the human race. Well, we cannot afford to antagonise a species we know nothing about," drawled a wide-eyed Kathryn Perkins, the communications officer, clearly worried about what her brash superior officer would say and do to the being from another world.

"We cannot squander this God-given opportunity to 'befriend' a more intelligent alien race of beings; it would be a sin not to cooperate and share what we know, that's all."

"One thing I'm not is an unfeeling fool; tactful I can and will be. Look, Kathryn, we have a good chance to better humanity on so many levels here and now," proffered the stoney-faced military man in response to what was a personal accusation aimed at him, though it was something he was probably guilty of if truth be known.

"Don't worry, I will be welcoming to our off-worldly spaceman. You're quite right, we must show interstellar detente towards one another as different species coexisting."

With that said they prepared to walk across to the support vehicle parked just outside the park's wide open wrought iron gates sixty metres away.

"You've read all of the reports, Kathryn, what do our experts have to say about that spaceship back there?" The experienced colonel asked as both he and his communications officer exited the portacabin and walked several steps then climbed into a waiting land rover.

"Well, for one thing, it's not metal; it is incredibly strong yet unbelievably tensile, like steel. It's perfect for the rigours of space flight and possible light-speed travel," informed the pretty blonde communications officer as the vehicle pulled away heading the short distance to the park gates and the much-anticipated date with destiny.

"In my opinion, we must find the secret of its manufacture and capabilities, that and everything else our ET friend can supply us with."

"Hmm, most interesting," purred her expectant commanding officer whilst the driver parked the land rover behind the mobile unit and turned off the engine. They had arrived.

Proceedings were halted by the shrill ringing tones from the cellphone in the colonel's top tunic pocket, which he deftly pulled out and switched on.

He listened with a blank expression as the subordinate officer explained the situation to him before proffering his response in a short terse growl.

"Get him here ASAP!"

"It seems our intrepid local boy has fallen from a tree and is unconscious as we speak. They are trying to wake him up on the way over here."

"What if he never comes round? What if the boy dies?"

The Mere thought that the alien-hosting child could end up dead taking their much sought-after extra-terrestrial away with him and did not bear thinking about it.

"He'll be alright, young kids are resilient and unbreakable. I was when I was his age. No, he will quickly recover believe me."

"Here they come now. Let's hope that you're right, Colonel, cos' I don't like penguins."

WHITE! Everything was white! A blurry white was the only thing John could see. Was he dead? The throbbing pain at the back of his head told him that he was not.

Slowly but surely, he began resurfacing from wherever he had returned from; dizziness affecting his focus but not his hearing, with two voices speaking at the same time.

"Wake up, John Philips, wake up!"

"How are you feeling, young man?" Two distinctly different voices proffered almost simultaneously, instantly confusing the bleary-eyed boy, especially as one seemed to be actually inside his head with him.

"You are awake at long last. Good. Unfortunately, we appear to have been captured and are prisoners."

"How is your head, my boy? You had quite a bad fall back there in the park."

"Cap…captured! I…I…I don…don't under…understand," stammered a thoroughly disorientated John Philips as his brain desperately attempted to make sense of events. Then it suddenly all came flooding back to him.

"Be careful what you reveal, John Philips, for both our sakes."

"It's okay, John, you are bound to feel disorientated after the time you've had along with our off-worldly visitor," purred a female voice in complete contrast to that of the deeply booming alien speaking a fraction of a second ahead of her, the twin conversations not helping at all.

"I…I feel sick! My…my head hurts like mad! Wh…why are you all staring at me?" An extremely weary John Philips groaned looking back up at a whole host of adults all staring down at him as if he himself were the alien.

"Hello, John, I'm Colonel Smithlington and I am in overall command of this military top-secret operation. Don't worry, young man, you are quite safe now," volunteered a tall, well-built, uniformed soldier, beaming down at him with what appeared to be scrambled egg on the rim of his peaked cap.

"We need to talk to the extra-terrestrial who we suspect has taken over your mind. To do that, we will have to render you into a more malleably fit state. Get him ready."

"No, John Philips, they are about to administer a drug that will render you unconscious so as to gain access to yours truly."

"This might hurt a little, young man, but then you will feel much better once you've taken a slight 'nap'," informed the pretty female soldier, her voice sounding nanoseconds ahead of the alien's, his attention fixed on the hypodermic syringe she was holding.

"Are you listening, John Philips? She is about to render you 'hors de combat' and unable to help yourself or me. Fight them, fight the desire to sleep for both our sakes."

"Lay perfectly still for me, won't you? Like I said, it may hurt a bit but soon you will be back home with your mum and dad. Here we go then."

"Wa…water! Can I have a drink of water, please?" The near to tears boy bleated, flinching as the needle sank slowly into his left arm, pain making him grimace as it did so; not that his nervous alien pal cared at all.

"Can you still focus, John Philips, you will quickly become very drowsy. Promise me that you will try to fight against it as I will do from within your primitive human mind."

"Here's your drink of water. Now, you've earned it for being so brave."

"Tha…thank you. Actually, I do feel a bit tiled, I—" droned a groggy-sounding John as the drug began to quickly take effect on him, slurring his voice in the process as he attempted to reply to the desperate alien.

"I…I…I wi…will d…d…do, I…I…"

"I think he's about ready, Colonel. Sleep if you want to, John. Go to sleep, young man, we need to speak to the space individual currently visiting this planet of ours. Sleep now, sleep."

"No, do not sleep, John Philips, fight against the urge, fight!" The stressed-out alien entity ordered knowing full well that it was losing the fight for control of the boy's mind as the drug did its job.

"I…I…I…" stammered a barely conscious John Philips as the sleep-inducing drug finally dragged him into the arms of Morpheus and a deep sleep took over.

"My name is Colonel Smithlington of this planet's US Airforce. I know that you can hear me inside the boy's mind which you entered from your space craft two nights ago," drawled the confident-sounding military man sitting directly in front of the unconscious boy. John's head was shrouded by high-tech equipment connecting him to a compute decoder and monitoring unit. "I, erm…'we' are your friends; we mean you no harm. You are a most welcomed guest on our planet Earth, but please speak with us so that we can learn from one another's species."

There was no response, the computer screen remaining blank much to the dismay of both him and the rest of the team stood around him on either side looking on.

"Please answer me, we want to help you and your race of beings, but only if we can communicate with each other. Please, there is so much to talk about," continued the experienced colonel, not prepared to take no for an answer, knowing full well that his job was on the line should it not all go to plan.

"I promise that we are not going to hurt or insult you in any way, shape or form, all we want to do is establish contact, that's all. Well, what do you say?"

Again nothing. Then moments later, the huge screen flashed into life, blindingly so, bursting with unusual light shapes, circles, and unimagined equations all at the same time.

Suddenly, the screen blacked out and was lit by a weird orange light as the computer returned to normal and began operating in earnest.

"My name is unimportant, Colonel Smithlington, and my visit here is peaceful. John Philips is quite safe just as long as 'I and he' remain unharmed and my vessel likewise," informed the reluctant alien having boosted the computer's ability to interpret, allowing it to speak in the language of the planet's indigenous population.

"Through the human child, I have learnt quite a lot about your planet and the species along with its needs, desires, beliefs and injustices."

"I don't mean to offend you but what can a small boy actually possibly know about any of those things you just spoke about, or anything at all for that matter," volunteered the unthinking colonel, completely dismissing the boy altogether; something that instantly annoyed the extra-terrestrial visitor in the process.

"John Philips was correct in that you Earthlings are a selfish, intolerant, troublesome race of beings, so desperate to reach the stars that you would steal my vessel to do so."

"Actually, not so much 'steal' as utilise its design and flight capabilities. Your spaceship is a God send as far as we human beings are concerned," responded a steely-eyed Colonel Smithlington without a trace of regret or apology, almost as if he was doing the right thing in commandeering the alien's spaceship from it.

"My vessel is effectively sealed and only I can physically open the portal, thus if you wish access, I suggest that you take me within view of it," proffered the miffed alien entity, thinking partly about the boy whose mind and body it was currently housing but mostly wanting an opportunity to escape the planet as soon as it possibly could. "The sooner that happens the better it should be for the Earth boy I speak to you from. Surely we must have joint co-operation between species, Colonel Smithlington?"

"I think that could be arranged, but first, there are many questions. To begin with, which star constellation do you call home? Surely not this one," rattled off the curious Air Force Special Tasks Officer in overall charge of Operation Retrieval. He like the others in the hushed confines of the ops unit vehicle desperate for answers.

"The constellation Plaeddisclazx along with my home world of Xvononipaume, the seventh planet from the bright star Creeaxixztaer. It will not appear on any of your existing Earth charts, see," explained the alien via the onscreen readout which burst into a series of three-dimensional images as it did so.

All jaws dropped open and stayed like that as image after image flashed across the screen, most never seen before by humanity but still they continued.

"Oh my God! Good God! I've never seen anything like it before. It's fantastic!" One of the gobsmacked air force technicians gushed who stood behind an equally wide-eyed Colonel Smithlington as all eyes bulged out as if on stalks at what they were seeing.

A moment later, the almost pyro-technical three-dimensional images ceased and once again were replaced by words as the alien in the unconscious boy's head spoke.

"I do not doubt that your 'God' would also find it mesmerising, but right now, I need to see my vessel, then you will see something equally amazing. How about it, Colonel Smithlington?"

The alien's request was hardly noticed following the non-Earthly technological display of three-dimensional star charts stretching out to areas of space utterly unknown to mankind.

"Yes, yes, I think we can manage that, especially now that we've protected it behind toughened PVC screens and fenced it in out of sight from our friend here. Open the side doors someone," droned a smug-looking Colonel Christopher Smithlington rubbing a large right hand over his balding head; the military officer fully confident that everything was under control.

"Colonel, I guess this is a close encounter people will always talk about, only this one must defy description, wouldn't you say so?" The white-coated technician drawled whilst pulling open the side door, instantly allowing a cold breeze to tousle his hair as he did so.

"Yes, Mister Dundonald, you might say that we have acquired a genuine extra-terrestrial, and a friendly one at that," cooed a chirpy, self-preening Colonel Smithlington rubbing both huge hands together in a manner that suggested that he was fully satisfied that they had the situation in hand.

"A visitor from beyond the stars themselves, a bona fide ET, it's a scientific dream come true, not to mention a feather in my own cap."

He was right. Together, he and his team had made history, not that anyone without clearance would ever know but nevertheless, it would do his future prospects no harm whatsoever, in fact, quite the opposite.

"I'm sorry, Mister and Missus Philips, but there is nothing I can do to help you right now. There's no telephone contact with the safety team at Hornsea at this moment in time," boomed the barrel-chested security guard sat behind a makeshift trestle table, as were two other high viz wearing men, both busy tapping away on separate computer keyboards.

"Please, when will there be any news? Our son, John, may be there at home, number 6 Trinity Road; he's only twelve," pleaded Anne Philips, keeping eye contact with the burly security guard as both she and her husband, Roger, tried desperately to get help in locating their son, John.

"Believe me, Mister and Missus Philips, I fully understand exactly what you must both be going through but I have my orders," admitted the sympathetic official with a nod of his thick bull neck; his words and expression doing little to ease the parental worry on their faces.

"What I can do for you is let you both know the second I hear anything about your son, anything at all, that's the best I can do for the time being."

"Thank you, I don't suppose you can tell us if they have managed to find and diffuse the atom bomb yet. It hasn't actually gone off yet, has it?" A dissatisfied Anne Philips quizzed, stating the obvious as far as the lack of an atomic explosion was concerned, but any news was something for them to hear.

"Don't worry, we've got the best bomb disposal experts in the world out there, but things can go unexpectantly wrong occasionally, not this time though, fear not and I'll keep you informed."

"Thanks, we'll look forward to hearing from you. Good night," drawled a disappointed Anne Philips whilst glancing at her equally miserable husband; the two standing and heading for the door, worry etched on both their tired-looking faces.

Apart from the thought of their only son being blown up and killed, there was also the fact that if the bomb actually did go off, it would destroy their home as well.

All they could do was wait for any news, anything at all. Why had they not sent John away from Hornsea and out of danger, it made no sense at all.

Unless, of course, something wasn't quite right out there, but what could that possibly be? Only time will tell…

"There's your spaceship. Not quite so cocky now, are we? Now you said that you would help get us into that thing, so do it now, my extra-terrestrial friend, right now," coaxed an ever-confident Colonel Smithlington knowing as he did that the shiny craft was now not boardable as far as the reasonably friendly alien entity in the boy's head was concerned.

There was no reply, the screen remained blank. Was the alien playing hard to get or was it simply unable to understand the position of check mate?

"Try again, Colonel, it seems that ET has sunk into its shell," volunteered another of the white-coated team members, there in an official capacity having worked with the same unit before and was very much part of the furniture.

"I know that you can hear me so don't play dumb. You promised that you would open the hatch and let us go inside your vessel, so kindly do just that for me."

As the colonel finished speaking, the computer screen flashed blindingly, forcing them to shield their eyes momentarily before settling back down as the alien responded.

"I will do as you ask but I need the boy, John Philips, to be conscious again. Will you do that for me, Colonel Smithlington?" The high-tech alien entity ventured via the unconscious boy's head; the request furrowing several brows including that of the colonel who suspected trickery at first.

"Well, Colonel, is bringing him back to the land of the living worth the price of a look inside my vessel? It sounds good to me. I do have my reservations but the pluses do outweigh the negatives. Administer the injection please, Susan."

They stood watching as the pretty air force woman administered the antidote to the still-unconscious boy. John instantly stirred as the drug began taking effect on him.

"John Phillips? John Phillips! Can you hear me, John Philips? Listen to my voice!"

Someone was speaking somewhere in the misty background as lights flickered kaleidoscopically where his vision should be. Then he heard it again.

"Tell me that you can hear me, John Philips? Talk! Please speak to me, it is important that you do."

"I…I…I ca…can h…hear you. I…I don…don't feel very well at all. I…I…" bleated back a painfully weak John Philips; his tongue dryer than sandpaper as was his throat, making it almost impossible to speak out loud. Then he recognised the voice talking to him.

"I bid you a fond farewell, my Earth friend. I hope that we meet again somewhere, some place in the ever-eventful future. It's a big, big collection of infinite possibilities out there," informed the alien entity as John struggled to understand what was going on and where he was.

"You never know your species might even make it to my planet with any luck. Goodbye, Earthling, I take good memories away into the stars with me. I am gone from here."

On saying that, there was a brilliantly bright pulse of light followed by a moment of unbelievable weightlessness, then nothing at all, nothing…

Chapter Seven

The first thing any of the team knew was a sudden flash of bright green light emanating from the makeshift hanger where the alien's spaceship was housed.

"Oh fuck, ET double-crossed us. It has gone back into its ship, the fucking lying bastard. It's about to take off, we're going to lose our precious alien. The MOD will have my pension as well as my balls if we let it get away!" The red-faced colonel screamed as the entire hanger lit with a tremendously bright white light, the ground vibrating beneath their feet as they stared helplessly on. "Do something, someone. We can't just stand here and let it take off back into the stars. We might not get another chance like this one."

"Colonel Smithlington, it's the boy. He's hardly breathing at all, with an extremely weak pulse. I think he might be dying," informed a woman's voice immediately behind the fuming colonel, making him spin on his heels as his troubles suddenly doubled. Surely they couldn't lose ET and the boy as well.

"No, no, that can't be right. Have you checked your equipment, there must be a fault in the system; double check it please," barked back her angry, miffed superior officer; his expression close to rage as he turned to see the disc-shaped vessel lift the entire hanger off the ground as they looked on.

"Damn it, there's nothing we can do! Wait a minute, get air command on it. We've shot it down once, we'll do it again. Connect me through right now," growled the infuriated air force officer shaking with rage at the thought of him being outsmarted by the off-world entity. He now wanted to blow out of the skies.

"Got them for you, Colonel. Its Wing Commander Thompsby. He wants to offer his congratulations on a job well done," voiced one of the two technicians sitting beside him, the message not what the upset Colonel wanted to hear at that moment in time as he snatched the telephone away from him and grunted into the receiver.

"Wing Commander, I need you to scramble a couple of jets to track down and destroy an escaping UFO still flying over east coast Ingle sea showing hostile intent; copy?"

"Copy that, Colonel, consider it done; over!" The agreeable wing commander announced in response to Colonel Smithlington's request, knowing full well that the special ops officer had full authority in all matters airborne.

"Send it right now, over and out!"

"It's about to go and so is the boy by the look of things. We need to get him to a hospital, Colonel, or he might die. He's slipping into a coma," trilled the attractive female medical officer having checked, then rechecked the young boy's vital signs, knowing as she did that everything was working as it should.

"Alright, call for an ambulance and we'll rush him over to the infirmary at Kingston. In the meantime, I want everyone out there keeping that spaceship down here on Earth!" A wild-eyed Colonel Smithlington bellowed without taking his eyes from the view outside as the makeshift hanger split in two allowing the trapped saucer its freedom.

"Damn it! Look after that boy, keep him alive for me. The rest of you outside with me, let's see if we can bring that double-crossing bastard back down to rejoin us, come on."

Once outside, they quickly realised that they were too late, the disc, along with its alien entity, had gone, shooting up out of Earth's atmosphere and away into space itself.

"Oh no! No! It's gone! We've lost the greatest prize in human history! I'm destined for 'Penguin duty' at the south pole now," spluttered a shattered Colonel Smithlington. The captured disc had disappeared altogether from view, as indeed had the hanger smashed in the impromptu take-off.

"Where is that fucking fighter jet I asked to be scrambled? I'll have Wing Commander Thompsby's bollocks for a pendant to frighten the penguins for this."

Just as he finished speaking, an almighty bang sounded from high above as the errant jet fighter broke the sound barrier in chase of the extra-terrestrial spacecraft.

"Colonel Smithlington, the boy is getting worse; he's fallen into a deep coma, there's nothing I can do for him now."

"Oh fuck! That's all we need. I presume that the ambulance is on its way?" The deflated Airforce officer groaned on hearing the news from his trustworthy medical officer. The press would have a field day once they discovered the truth about all this.

"What about the young boy, Colonel? He's extremely weak, not to mention very slow breathing. We need that thing here immediately or he might not make it."

"I hope that it is fitted with a straight jacket because I must have been madly trusting that ET to do the right thing," droned the officer in sole charge of the spacecraft recovery, only to lose it altogether thanks to his own stupidity as he stood staring upwards at where the saucer had departed.

All was lost as far as both he and his military career were concerned. After today's debacle, he'd be lucky to run an on-base ice cream concession stall in future.

All was indeed lost…

Take-off had been smoothly rewarding once the vessel broke free from its restraints, quickly leaving the planet's nitrogen-rich atmosphere without any problems.

The Earth boy, John Philips, was still fresh in its thoughts as the ship shot past the planet's single moon to begin the journey to his next destination.

It had been a dangerous yet strangely exhilarating visit to the third planet from 'sol', its bright sun, the entire solar system flashing past as the ship entered light leap heading for the Andromeda galaxy.

His chosen destination was far beyond Andromeda, three more galaxies to a planet called Yybaeakloed, the fourteenth circling the star Pikttuumbaue for welcomed R&R.

The horrendous business back on the planet Earth had been a real eye-opener, having been forced to emergency eject into the mind of a young boy looking on.

That Earth boy taught him more about the human condition as far as its greedy, unscrupulous adults were concerned than all his previous visits had; far more.

It had been a taste of humanity unenjoyable in the extreme, Earth was avoided by most species throughout the mega galaxy of planets, fearing contamination of mind, body, and soul.

To him, Earthlings were mostly a self-centred race of beings; not all of them, somewhere honest, hard-working subjects, but the majority were not.

What people on Earth wanted most was the secret surrounding deep space travel, something as yet unavailable to them but for how much longer…

With Earth well and truly behind him, he could relax and enjoy the forthcoming journey safe in the knowledge that he'd never ever set feet on Earth again.

With his vessel engaged fully in a light leap manoeuvre, he'd soon arrive at the six-mooned planet and detoxify his life expectancy unit in unbelievably relaxed surroundings.

Maybe, others of his species of space travellers would be on Yybaeakloed to greet and stroll with him, maybe not, but it would be blissfully peaceful after his visit to Earth.

"I'm sorry to have to tell you this but your son, John, is in a deeply troubling coma. We have no idea as of yet as to how long it will last, or if he'll ever come out of it," informed the tall bearded doctor, all the while watching the expressions on the faces of Gloria and Roger Philips as they drank in the bad news about their son, John.

"Then again, I suppose it's hardly surprising following the ordeal he must have gone through. Still, we are monitoring his vital details. Any questions?"

"What ordeal are you talking about here?" A furrow-browed Gloria wanted to know, tears well on the way as she stared back in utter bemusement, as did her equally baffled husband stood beside her.

"Well, to be perfectly honest with you, I don't have all of the facts only that he may have gotten too close to the bomb they managed to get up from the freshwater lake," volunteered the white-coated doctor in all sincerity, his word not what either parent wanted to hear in the circumstances but had no choice in the matter.

"All I can surmise is that perhaps the atomic bomb's cover plate came loose and leaked, your son may well have encountered a weak dose of radiation poisoning."

"He is going to make it, isn't he? John is quite a strong-willed boy you know." A troubled Roger Philips asked, seeing his wife nodding her head in agreeance of his question; one they both needed a reply to in a positive vein.

"It's impossible to say, Mister Philips. All we can do is to look after him as best we can letting nature take its course. It's all we can do," droned the smiling doctor, concern evident in his practiced manner; one he hoped would suitably placate the boy's worried parents as best he could in the circumstances.

"Surely there must be something you can do for our son?"

"I'm sorry, Mister Philips, but all we can do now is to wait it out. Don't worry, we'll look after him," admitted Doctor Rickmanswhite, staring as they were down at the tiny, lifeless boy laying in a death-like state, surrounded by an array of pipes, tubes, and electrical equipment.

"Do you happen to know whether or not they managed to defuse the bomb that's kept Hornsea closed all this time?" A teary-eyed Gloria Philips asked without removing her gaze from her unmoving son, a constant beeping noise irritating her as it monitored the child's condition.

"Again, I do not know. It's all being kept so very hush-hush, you know, military matters and all that, but I feel sure that they'll know exactly what they are doing out there," proffered the world-weary doctor checking his wrist watch as he did so having a previous appointment at the other part of the hospital and was already late.

"Believe me, Hornsea will still be there by the time they allow you back there. In the meantime, I suggest that you pray for him and let God take it from there. Hey, I've got to go, goodbye."

"Thank you, Doctor, and we appreciate everything you've done, goodbye."

Together, they watched a tired-looking Doctor Rickmanswhite stroll from the room, leaving them alone with their comatose son in the noisy hospital observation unit.

"Oh God, Roger! What on Earth are we going to do now?" A thoroughly devastated Gloria Philips exclaimed between sobs of despair, her fears shared in equal measure by her husband as they peered down at the horizontal boy.

They both knew that the doctor had been correct and that the only thing they could do was sit and wait. Hopefully, he would come back to them sooner rather than later.

The planet Yybaeakloed was a low gravity paradise as far as his race of beings was concerned, with wide deserts and an over-abundance of enormous lakes and seas as well.

It would be the perfect place to unwind after his unnecessary but remarkably engaging coexistence on Earth, which coupled with a danger-filled escape into space left a scar he needed to have soothed out of his bio-systems.

This particular planet was unique with its seven moolis and oval ring system, perfect for him to fully mind relax whilst strolling along the living lake of Wizwazwere.

The waters of the lake were not liquid but were made up of unimaginably countless creatures called 'Wizwerzeez', tiny individually but oceanesque in vast numbers.

As he made yet another slow lap of its mighty shores, he thought he heard a voice somewhere deep inside the recesses of his mind, and then it stopped.

The lake was as usual undulating with microscopic energy, it was incredibly soothing. Then two things happened simultaneously causing his emotions to hiccup with mixed incredulation.

Suddenly, without warning, the tiny 'Wizwereez' linked on and leapt upwards to form a colossal three-dimensional shape in mid-air before slowly cascading down again.

It happened only when six of the planet's seven moons were perfectly aligned. It was a truly magnificent display, but the spectacle was interrupted by a tiny voice.

"Wh…where am I?" A voice other than his own and in a language unknown to him as well droned. It was faint but audible. Could it be a memory hiccup after all?

"Where am I? Mum, Dad, I don't understand! Somebody help me please!"

There it was again, he mused to himself as the planet's cryo-energy waves seeped into his body and mind through each and every single pore, healing him as they did so.

The unpleasant incident on Sol's third planet had taken its toll on his inner psyche, so much so that he needed to recharge himself before going back out into the cosmos again.

"It's dark, so very dark! Am I dead? Why is everything so very different?"

It sounds like John Philips; yet how can that be? Surely he is back on the Earth where I left him. Tell me that I have not gone space senile already, mused the frowning ZSarrboddliiien as yet again the familiar voice sounded, seemingly in an area of his own mind, a place inhabited only by fleeting moments but nothing else.

"H…help me, someone! I want to see my family again, please. I…I don't like it here, I…"

"By the Jong missing peoples of Evacu 8, John Phillips? It cannot be. John Philips? By Zllandeaopia! Answer me if you are truly there, my young Earth friend," blurted the surprised tri-pede, its crinkling forehead and stunned expression bearing testament to just how shocking the situation was if it turned out to be true.

"John Philips? Can you hear me, John Philips? John Philips, it's me, remember, back on your own home planet? Why can't you understand me at all?"

"There's a strange, high-pitched series of clicks and beeps going on all around me. Where am I? Help me, someone! Can't you hear me at all?"

It suddenly dawned on the tri-pedal visitor that whilst he was speaking in his own language the Earth child was listening in its own mother tongue, an adjustment needed to be made.

"Can you hear me now, John Philips? If you can, then it is I who am finding it difficult to understand what has happened."

"Whe…where am I? And where on Earth are you?" The clearly disorientated boy bleated from within the alien's uncluttered mind; his question troubling his equally shocked host as he continued his stress-relieving stroll.

"I, or rather we, are on the planet Yybaekloed and not on your Earth at all. I am at a loss as to how this could possibly have happened."

"Wha…what has happened?"

"The only explanation available is that I must have taken your essence away with me when I re-entered my vessel. You are lucky to remain alive, John Philips."

"Planet Yybag…erm Yybakl…whatever you called it, where is that in relation to my planet?" A mystified John Philips replied, the human boy finding it hard to comprehend the situation. Was he being the victim of a rather cruel practical joke?

"Many, many thousands of your planet's light years, in a far-flung galaxy. Sorry, John Philips, I really am."

"But what about my home, my planet, my parents? They…they'll be worried about me as I am for them," stammered the near to tears youngster from the depths of the tri-pede's huge brain. John was hoping that this was simply a bad dream and he would wake up any moment now.

"That's it! It's a dream! I'm in bed back at home, you're not really here. Yes, that's it." John chirped having convinced himself in an instant, only for his host to shatter his illusions once and for all.

"Sorry, John Philips, but this is no dream you are in. We are in another star constellation from your own solar system. You know that I cannot lie or tell untruths."

There was an ominous silence from the young Earth boy as he drank in the seemingly impossible. Surely such a thing was in the realms of science fiction, or were they?

"John Philips? I know you can hear me, John Philips, I did not deliberately mean to bring you here with me, you must have teleported into my vessel with me back on Earth," volunteered the knowledgeable extra-terrestrial being, already working out exactly how to deal with the situation forced on it by circumstances not of its choosing.

"It's…it's not possible, it can't be," announced a thoroughly perplexed John Philips, doing his level best to wrap his head around what the ET was telling him, but it was hard work all the same.

"Everything is possible until proved impossible, John Philips. Your people are finding that out for themselves, are they not? But it's early days yet for humanity," droned the informative space being whilst gazing at the sea of microscopically small creatures making up the living lake to his left, breathing in the life-giving properties they expelled as he did so.

"Oh, you're not as backwards thinking as a species as you've been told to believe, with gravity skim saucers, moon bases, alien contacts, miracle cures."

"We did land on the moon, I remember learning about it at boarding school. Then again, my dad did say that no, they did not, it was all a gigantic hoax," replied the small boy's voice in his head, sounding distant but Merely millimetres away. John's comments were not known by his host who could not respond to them.

"I know nothing of your Earthly conspiracies, John Philips, but what I do know is that we'll just have to get you back there again, won't we?"

"Ca…can you really get me back home to Earth? My parents will be worried sick about me," gushed a suddenly animated John Philips, sounding glad to be able to actually return to his home on Earth. But how long would it take to get back there?

"Will I be still alive or am I dead back on Earth?"

"Do not fear, John Philips. By my reckoning, your physical body will be in a comatose condition and will remain that way until you awaken," informed the knowledgeable tri-pede, seemingly fully aware of how humanity functioned, just as well seeing as how he knew absolutely nothing at all about it himself.

"But we have a big problem. The longer you are in the coma, the more they are likely to assume that you are brain dead and switch the machine off that is keeping you alive."

"We…we've got to get going, the sooner the better, before they turn me off altogether," blurted the frightened boy. John was suddenly worried that by the time he got back to Earth, there would be no body to return to. A terrifying prospect indeed.

"Trust me, John Philips, I will get you back to your planet long before that takes place, but first, my vessel is undergoing treatment on its prizmic calibration unit," trilled the confident-sounding alien being; it's comforting words improving John's overall condition but not dampening his desire to go back home to his parents.

"It needs its core to be recentred. Once that is achieved, we can be on our way. Meanwhilst, allow yourself to enjoy the sights you see while you can."

"How about showing me where we are right now?" A hopeful John Philips ventured wanting nothing more than to catch a brief glimpse of another world to take back to Earth with him if possible.

"Sorry, Doctor, but it's our son, John. He's not in his room. Can you tell us what happened to him?" A worried-looking Gloria Philips quizzed, who had turned up at the hospital to visit their son, John, along with her husband only to find his room empty, their offspring gone.

"Did you not get my email? Your son stopped breathing last night so we were forced to place him in an iron lung so that we can better monitor his progress, if any," revealed an unsmiling Doctor Rickmanswhite in no uncertain terms as the boy's startled parents listened on, both horrified by what they were hearing as he continued.

"I'm afraid John's brain patterns and life signs are fading; a little too quickly at present, unless he comes out of it in the next day or two, well…"

"Oh no! No! This can't be happening! Not to us!" The boy's frowning father blurted, both parents utterly distraught and close to tears at the chilling thought of losing their only son.

"He…he will recover, won't he, Doctor?" A red-eyed Gloria Philips pleaded, her legs suddenly gelatinous as the devastating news thumped into her like a fist blow; her emotions already shattered, as were her husband's as well.

"Well, we could try and see if he responds to your voices. You never know, it might just succeed in bringing him back to reality. It's got to be worth a shot, what do you say?"

"Yes, yes, let's do that. Where is he?"

On saying that, Doctor Rickmanswhite led the red-eyed couple along a fairly busy corridor and in through a lock-coded set of doors, swiping his security badge to get in.

Only John's head remained visible as he lay inside a bulky, elongated, sarcophagus-style machine amidst a collection of beeps and whooshing sounds as they looked on.

"Oh my God!" Both parents gasped simultaneously on catching sight of their near-death offspring, the machine surrounding him hissed noisily as it did the boy's breathing for him.

"Go on, talk to him, say anything but let him know that it is his parents talking."

They did just that, announcing themselves to him somewhat self-consciously, chatting away as if on the telephone, their son laying unmoving in the iron lung as they did so.

"Can we stay with him for a bit longer please, Doctor?" The boy's anxious mother asked blinking away the tears at the sound of her husband's voice competing with the machine's ever-present noises as it kept their son alive and breathing.

"Alright but not too long though because we've still got one or two more tests to do. The nurse will tell you when it's time to leave, goodbye."

"Thank you, Doctor, I'm sure that John will hear us and wake up," proffered a thankful Gloria Philips as the doctor strolled from the room leaving the Philips to try to reawaken their comatose son laying inside the iron lung.

"John, it's mum and dad! We're here for you, son! John! We are here! John! John! John!"

"Well, Colonel Smithlington, you have lost both the flying saucer and its alien pilot. What happened out there?" The third of three officious-looking MOD men sent to urgently debrief the humiliated RAF officer in a judge and jury style meeting growled.

"A clever, creative ET coupled with a knowledgeable local boy. ET shot from the spaceship and hitched a ride inside his mind. The rest is in my report," remarked the unsmiling colonel having already submitted a full report for the three-man committee to browse prior to the oral investigation and inquest into the incident.

"Tell us, Colonel, how did a twelve year old boy outwit and outsmart that team of yours, and how did he enter and elude you from the outset?" The younger of the sour-faced trio sat across from him quizzed, his expression one of dislike having looked forward to this moment for quite some time.

"Firstly, the kid was local and knew the town like the back of his hand. Second, he inherited a super intellect thus giving him the drop on us most of the time."

"Colonel Smithlington, it says here that you caught then lost the boy and alien not once but twice, tell us how to please," chirped the third man in the row facing him; a fat, sweating individual badly in need of a decent diet from the look of him, mused the unamused RAF Special Forces Officer.

"Erm, the first time we locked the drugged boy inside one of the portacabins at the Mere-side peninsula, only for him to climb out through an overhead skylight duct," admitted a slightly embarrassed Colonel Smithlington, his tone betraying the sense of shame at his failure to do his job and secure the spaceship and its pilot.

"The second time we drugged the boy to allow us to converse with the alien hiding in his head, only for it to trick us into waking the boy up, then it got back to its ship and escaped into outer space."

"We disagree, Colonel, I for one believe that you could have done plenty of things to keep both of them in our grasp. Instead, you've made us a laughing stock," barked the MOD man between his two colleagues, anger flashing across his features as the severity of the colonel's acutely monumental loss kicked in.

"I agree that it is a massive loss but we were dealing with vastly superior intelligence here. Okay, it was via a small boy, nevertheless, they outthought us," blustered a rapidly reddening Colonel Smithlington, the RAF officer beginning to bristle with anger as his forthcoming and irreversible crucifixion drew ever closer.

"Anyhow, all the safeguards were in place, infrared night-vision patrols plus the chopper with ultraviolet sweeps, yet still the boy sneaked past them all."

"Yes, he did, didn't he? Leaving us with no flying saucer, no alien spaceman, a child in a coma who might die, and us with only egg on our faces as a result," countered Sir Vivian Bloomsbottom with a snotty sneer, staring down his long nose at the frowning colonel from one end of the trio as the RAF officer squirmed uncomfortably back at him. "It also leaves us in quite a predicament. It's far too late to deny that it ever happened what with satellite technology, they'll have seen everything."

"Right then, let's get down to the nitty-gritty here, shall we, gentlemen? Where do we go from here?" The under-pressure RAF officer wanted to know attempting to turn the tables on the three-man posse sent there to take his balls back with them.

"Go from here? We, erm, we blame you of course for the loss of the spaceship and occupant. I for one would be interested in why you appear so calm in the circumstances."

"I'm not panicking because I believe that all is not lost. Yes, I managed to lose the saucer and alien pilot, but what if I told you that I might be able to recapture it, what then?"

The statement by Colonel Smithlington made the trio opposite stare with wide-eyed incredulation at the unruffled RAF man sat gazing confidently back at them.

"Colonel Smithlington, are you on any strong medication that you feel you want to tell us about because you are on extremely thin ice right now?" Ex-Major General Karnabby commented, the first of the three men to find his voice following the shocking statement by the RAF Special Forces Officer staring confidently back at them.

"No, Sir, I'm not on drugs. What I am saying to you is that I have a theory of my own that whilst sounding unbelievable to you, may just turn out to be true. Shall I carry on, gentlemen?"

The three men sitting across from him nodded simultaneously but remained silent, each wearing a furrow-browed expression as the colonel began speaking.

"The way I see it when the alien entity zinged its way into its ship and its own body, it inadvertently took the boy's life force or spirit in there with it."

The looks on the trio of officials' faces were a picture of intrigued bafflement coupled with mesmerised disbelief as they drank in the colonel's utterly incredible story.

"If I'm right, and I believe that I am, that is the reason for the boy's sudden lapse into a coma, thus once the alien discovers this, he will be forced to bring him back here."

"Tha…that's utterly preposterous! Then again, it does say quite a lot about the situation we now find ourselves in right now viz a viz the boy's near-to-death coma, doesn't it?" The twinkly-eyed Sir Vivian rattled off in response to a quite extraordinary tale; one he was warming to with each passing moment as the other two men to his left listened on.

"Erm…supposing you are correct in your crazy assumptions, what do you propose doing about it, Colonel, if anything?" An unsmiling Ex-Major General Karnabby grilled with a nod of agreeance towards his fellow inquisitor having heard Sir Vivian's comments a moment earlier.

"We are going to set up a long-range radar look out for its approach, then once it is on the scanner, we wait until it's within our atmosphere, then shoot it down again."

"You do know what will happen to you should you fail to bag it a second time, don't you, Colonel Smithlington?" The portly MOD man on the right-hand side of the trio snorted; the threat was very real as far as his own military career was concerned, he'd be posted to Antarctica never to return.

"Yes, but let's hope that it never comes to that. Have no fear, gentlemen, I'll get you your flying saucer and alien occupant if it's the last thing I do."

With those words ringing in their ears, the meeting ended, as did all thoughts of emperor penguins. He'd be ready next time, no mistake.

Chapter Eight

"Good news, John Philips, get ready because we are about to leave this planetary system and head for your world."

He heard the alien's voice boom at him as he watched its huge fingers skim across a vaguely familiar control panel, one or two markings like Egyptian hieroglyphics to him.

"Good! Can't wait to get back home again. Not that I haven't enjoyed my time here with you, of course. How long will it take to reach Earth?"

"The journey to your solar system will take one of your Earth days, and then you will be reacquainted with your own body; that is if your adult population do not become aggressive again."

"I hope we will get there in time for my awakening and not my funeral. I want to see mum and dad smiling happily, not in floods of tears crying their eyes out," remarked the optimistic boy from the alien beings frontal lobe, having learnt how to do so by trial and error, annoying his host no end in the process.

"You can eject your human eyes, can you, John Philips? I did not know that about your species," queried the alien in all seriousness; the comment bringing a chuckle to the disembodied human child's voice as he attempted to explain the complexities of human sayings to a non-human.

"No, our eyes don't eject, they are fixed into our heads. It means that we cry so much that it appears that way. Maybe I didn't explain that correctly after all."

"Do not worry yourself, John Philips, I have been on your planet on many, many occasions, so I think I know you humans a little bit at least," volunteered his confident host with several clicking sounds and noises John worked out were akin to human laughter, something that adhered it to him in a nice way.

"If you lost your tendency and need for outright acts of extreme genocide and violent atrocities, we might even be able to communicate and meet up in the future."

John did not reply, there was no need, the alien had humanity bang to rights as far as their need to fight and destroy their enemies was concerned, history would judge.

Peace and harmony were the alien's words, the necessity not to harm any other life forms was built into their genome; kill only if all else fails, cool rules.

He had still not seen a full reflection of his host but knew that it had three legs and massive hands, it loped but could sprint if need be; not it really mattered.

Together, they had planet-hopped from one world to the next as his host checked on both its vessel and its own pleasures, not minding that he was inside its mighty brain.

The planet it enjoyed the most turned out to be a neuroworld, one created by the thoughts of the person using it, in this case, his alien host.

It was quite literally mind-controlled, turned instantly into whatever was required via a neuron translator picked up from a long way away.

This particular alien loved deserts and lakes, mile upon mile of soft almost liquid sand, perfect for the tri-pede being to wobble along lost in its own thoughts.

The sand particles were deep and seemingly alive, shimmering and glistening like water. The alien was doing a Jesus stroll but on a different planet altogether.

The Earth boy had absolutely no idea as to where they were in relation to the alien spaceship they had arrived there in; all he could do was to await the return journey.

One moment they were strolling through a windstorm of oily mud particles, the next lying flat out amidst a forest of mind-soothing crystals glowing and flowing opaquely all around.

"What are these things, sculptures or something?" John found himself wanting to know as the fiery columns began glowing in intensity, seemingly moving ever closer to them as the alien lay basking in the light.

"They are the residents of the planet. They are feasting on my accumulated negativity and have never encountered any of your species before. They welcome you, John Philips."

"Thank them for me, please, won't you?" The fascinated human child responded utilising the alien's senses to better understand the creatures surrounding him in his erstwhile mindset.

"By the way, would it be alright if I used your optics once we entered my own solar system? I'd like to see it first-hand as we approach my home planet."

"My vessel has no need for portals but I will neutralise the entire front of the craft thus you will have your fill of what is there for you to gaze on," complied the generous alien, leaving John guessing as to what 'neutralising the vessel' actually entailed. Would a screen be lowered? Perhaps not.

He would soon find out as the return journey began in earnest; the alien pilot reaching the next star constellation in minutes instead of hours as John had expected.

"Wow! I bet this spaceship can go very fast compared to the machines back on my planet!" The wide-eyed boy gushed from within the alien's concentrating mind as a multitude of colours shuddered and merged together as they flashed through it at incredible speed.

"Mine and many other worlds have managed to harness the power of the quark tachyon neutrino interchange of energies, a concept still not fully understood as we speak," volunteered his informative host as they continued the journey onwards, his explanation lost on the twelve year old earth boy lodged in the alien's brain.

"At the moment, we are closing in on what your people call the Andromeda galaxy, known by other races as Aamooggmllerx, home of the 'Preeaadomm' race of giants."

"I…I'll take your word for that. Any chance of me being able to see the journey from now on?" John asked having dismissed the technical information as to how the spaceship around them was powered as not his place to know, he was only twelve.

On saying that, the alien pilot reached out and waved a flat finger across a section of the control panel in front of it, instantly melting away the entire body of the vessel around them.

As far as the shocked boy could tell, the ship had disappeared altogether leaving them floating at incredible speed amongst a sea of stars. Where had the walls gone?

It was both breathtakingly beautiful yet frighteningly impossible as sudden panic hit him. John felt extremely disorientated, his mind unable to accept what was happening.

"Wha…what's going on? I…I…I…"

"Calm down, you are quite safe, John Philips. Discipline your mind, tell your inner self that no harm can befall you whilst aboard this vessel of mine," informed the experienced alien as John peered out via its wide-set eyes, seeing pinpoints of light zig-zagging past without ever endangering the ship or them in the process.

"Believe me, we are safely enveloped inside the vessel, only I have neutralised the outer and inner hulls in order for you to view what is of interest to you."

"Ye…yes, I…erm, I see tha…that! I…I…" stammered the goggle-eyed human boy finding himself slowly but surely growing accustomed to seeing sights never before seen by humanity, yet here he was.

"We are about to pass through your Andromeda galaxy so be prepared to be surprised by what you see."

On saying that, the spaceship began slowing as they swept into a gaseous swarm of sparkling particles, onto a scene that made John instantly smile inside.

At the very centre of the cloud were what he thought at first were angel-winged creatures flying in formation like birds, only these weren't angels at all but were made of metal.

"Hey, they are angels, aren't they?" The breathlessly exhilarated boy exclaimed whilst gazing out at the sight through the eyes of his experienced alien host, quick to point out their real identity to him.

"Not exactly, John Philips, they are Merely playful Meeotyds feeding. As they have fun, they usually mimic what your people refer to as shooting stars."

"Shooting stars eh! I think I saw one of those once back at my boarding school. Perhaps it was one of those things out there."

"Perhaps, John Philips, but we cannot remain here for too long in case they stop feeding and shoot away in all directions."

At that very moment, the metallic-looking creatures launched themselves outwards, exploding like a gigantic firework, sending sparks shooting everywhere at once.

"By Reegooheal's name! They make quite a spectacle when disturbed, agreed, John Philips?"

"Y…yes! Yes, they do! Where have they all gone?" A questioning John bleated, clearly impressed by the sight he had just witnessed; one possibly never to be seen by another person from planet Earth. A unique experience indeed.
"See that cluster of stars over to our right, they live on one of the moons of the eighteenth planet there. Sorry, but I cannot recall its name at present, John Philips," revealed the somewhat apologetic alien as it sped the vessel out of the

cloud cluster towards the very centre of the galaxy whilst John stared excitedly on.

"We should have enough time for me to take a quick detour to check something out. Don't worry, John Philips, we'll get you to Earth in plenty of time, agreed?"

John had little choice but to go with the alien's flow so to speak, enjoying the journey as he was it seemed stupid not to allow his host to do his own thing.

With deft accuracy and skill, the alien guided his vessel into and through a series of moons encircling a bright purple planet like an enormous pinball machine.

Finally, the clever alien landed on a pre-determined area and ran its enormous hands across the control panel markings that switched everything off.

With speed John found slightly disturbing, the alien exited the spaceship along with his human mind guest, heading for one of several low domes and walking on inside.

Instead of being in a cold, empty barrowesque hall, they had entered a massive indoor city, one complete with a busy market and hundreds of shops of one kind or another.

With his human passenger looking on, the alien reached a long downward drop and simply stepped over the edge, instantly falling only to slow to a gravity-held descent.

"He...hey! We...we're falling!"

"Don't worry, Earthling; we are in a gravity brake system, we cannot be hurt. I need to speak to a friend of my people, then on to your own planet; bear with me."

John remained silent. The Earth boy was quite enjoying the way they were floating downwards to the alien's destination below in the gloomy depths.

A moment later, they stopped and the alien waddled off onto a wide platform which suddenly sped away at what to John seemed incredibly fast.

No sooner had they set off, the platform began slowing, then pulled to a halt, allowing the confident alien to flick at an area of wall which slid silently open.

Once through the opening, they turned left only for John to realise that they were strolling along a narrow corridor that spanned several unbelievably tall buildings.

Each building must have been half a mile wide and at least a mile tall, the sight making him gasp with amazement. Then the alien glanced upwards.

"We are currently fourteen miles beneath the surface of the planet and three hundred miles away from my vessel. Is this a bit like your own dwelling places, John Philips?" His host in mid-waddle inquired. The sight overhead was truly staggering, revealing that the planet had been honeycombed, super excavated on a scale humans could only dream about.

The surface ceiling was nowhere to be seen to the naked eye, only fantastically ginormous dwelling places filled the sky in all directions he looked around him.

"There aren't any places like this on Earth. Skyscrapers yes, but not on this scale. This is unbelievable, magnificent. It's a council's worst nightmare," joked the admiring twelve year old boy as his host arrived at what to John was a dead end, only for the alien to wave its big right hand in a weird mid-air signal and wait.

Instantly, he and a startled John were lifted off the ground and found themselves floating as if on an invisible hand the short distance to the next walkway along.

"Oh my God! This technology is way beyond what we have back on Earth. It's staggering!" John groaned, more to himself than anything else, hearing the series of clicks and hisses he knew were laughter from his host on hearing the human boy's words of admiration.

"They know how to build them on this planet, John Philips, or rather inside them, you had better remain silent whilst I conduct my business, my young Earth friend," announced the clever, resourceful alien tri-pede as they got to a blank section of walkway and stopped. Nothing was visible as far as John could detect but his host knew different.

"Do not impede my thought stream or the powers that may suspect me of smuggling person contraband across the continuum contrary to space rules, agreed?"

"Space rules? You don't mean that you have people policing the cosmos, do you?" The disbelieving human child exclaimed, his tone full of mock sarcasm; something his host did not understand as it made two hand gestures in mid-air.

"Just keep quiet and we will soon be on our way to your own solar system. Here we go, John Philips."

The moment it finished speaking, they were lit up by a flash of brilliant orange light, the walkway suddenly lurching away to be replaced by a long well-lit room.

John bit his non-existent lip as the realisation of what had just taken place struck him; the alien had somehow been beamed from one place to another in the blink of an eye. One minute his host was on the walkway, the next he wasn't, only he had not moved, but rather the room he now stood in had come to him.

To John, it was as fantastically technical as it was completely out of human capabilities to replicate; so much so that he made a mental note to ask how it worked later on.

With his mind filled with thoughts of technical wizardry, he did as requested remaining still and quiet as the weird alien conversation got underway.

It was complete and utter gobbledegook as far as John could make out, a long series of high-pitched whistles followed by low guttural grunts and clicks.

Thankfully, it did not last very long, one moment the two non-human creatures were deep in alien talk, the next waddling along the narrow unprotected walkway again.

"Good news, John Philips, your planet has been selected by an intergalactic committee to be nominated for possible friendly integration visits," boomed his gregarious host, having suddenly found his voice as they boarded the wide platform and prepared for what would be a speedy return back to their original start point.

"I have voted for it not to be included on the list and for very good reason; you are not yet ready for contact by superior technologies. Do you agree?"

"I suppose I have little choice but to agree with you there judging by the way they treated you when they wanted your ship and technology on my planet," admitted a disproportionately frank and honest John having recalled to mind the lengths adults back on Earth were prepared to go to steal someone else's secrets.

"A very wise statement from someone so very young, John Philips, with any luck, you will go far on your planet. Let us hope so, my impetuous Earth child friend," commented his complementary alien mind host as the platform ride slowed to a halt having completed the three-hundred-mile journey in the blink of an eye.

"But first, we still have to get you back home and into the body that awaits you along with your parents. You might surprise one or two doctors as well with your remarkable recovery."

With that, the buoyant alien stepped from the platform, made a complex movement with one hand, and then waddled confidently in through a wide unlit archway.

The moment it did so, it was caught in an incredibly strong updraught, one that instantly yanked him into the air faster than John thought possible to do so.

Faster than a speeding bullet, they flew upwards inside the gravity-controlled vacuum lift, arriving seconds later back up on the planet's surface.

With its business completed, the alien quickly made its way back to its waiting vessel and once securely belted in, took off, exiting the planet's atmosphere en route to planet Earth.

"Well, John Philips, time to take you home to your own world. Soon you will not even remember any of this journey, probably thinking it simply as a bad dream."

"No, definitely not. I'll always remember you. Maybe we'll meet up again if our paths cross, you never know," retorted John from the alien's frontal lobe, having seen enough wonders to know that his own race of humans could learn a lot from his host's attitude to life's wonderments.

Neither one spoke as the vessel shot through the Andromeda galaxy and on towards the one containing Earth's solar system and his own comatose, near-death, body.

"What'll we do if we get there too late and they cannot wake me up at all?"

John wanted to know, breaking the silence between them just as his host noticed something out in the darkness surrounding the Earth-bound spaceship.

"Look over to our right and tell me what you see, John Philips. Let's see how observant you humans can be."

"What? Where? I don't see anything!" The young boy exclaimed, utilising the clever alien's bulging eyes to gaze out at the almost empty void around the vessel to see only the vast blackness of space in that direction.

"You see nothing, do you not? Yet if I turn on the infrared scanner, look again, John Philips, gaze in wonder!"

He looked on as his alien host waved its left hand over the lower area of his unreadable set of hieroglyphicesque symbols; then everything changed.

"How about now, John Philips?"

As his host spoke, the entire contents of space outside altered, illuminating what was not there a moment earlier as the young boy gazed out in open-mouthed stupefaction.

"Oh my God!" A wide-eyed John Philips husked, having caught sight of what was out there; a truly enormous metal spaceship filled the entire upper half of space itself.

"What? What the heck is it?"

John heard himself ask as they continued beneath the colossal spaceship, minutes ticking by as the unbelievably huge, city-sized vessel flew onwards overhead.

"That, John Philips, is an Xlyyslyybuum cargo vessel bound for a planet even I cannot pronounce in the Kvvooquallwea star system, millions of your light years from here," trilled the knowledgeable alien as the ginormous space vessel finally concluded, passing them by and allowing the usual pinpricks of stars to once more spill into view.

"It…it's massive! I've never seen anything as big as that where I come from," replied the truly overawed Earth boy as the undeniably huge cargo ship began slowly disappearing from view behind them into the darkness of deep space.

"That is Merely a petite vessel, the much bigger ones carry entire planetary systems from one place to another should that be required of them," informed his ultra-genial host as the journey continued onwards, the stars beginning to form much brighter, closer clusters as they approached the Milky Way galaxy.

"We are almost at your solar system, John Philips, my vessel's instruments tell me that most of the nine planets are almost close to alignment," volunteered the alien pilot as John peered out from his host's eyes, seeing things in a strangely off-world perspective; not that it mattered to his ultra-stimulated mind.

"We should have time for a closer look at several of them prior to arriving at the third one from Sol. What do you say, my Earth-bound young friend?"

"Yes, of course, I do. How long until we reach the planet we call Pluto?"

"What your people call the outer planet is exactly seven of your Earth minutes away. I believe that you, John Philips, are the first human to see it up close."

John did not reply straight away, instead wondering just what his friends and parents would think and say; perhaps they would suggest that it was Merely a dream whilst in the coma.

"I would love to do just that."

"Very well, John Philips. Pluto, here we come. You'll be going where no man has gone before if you pardon the Earth-bound pun from one of your television shows."

"Hey, that's not bad. Now I know even aliens watch sci-fi programs on the telly; well done," acknowledged the alien-housed earth boy suddenly engaged in what could only be called first-hand fun and spectacle unique to anyone else in human history.

Two minutes later, they officially entered the solar system, something he was the first to do, not that anyone would ever believe it of him.

"There is the planet you call Pluto, John Philips. I will take us as low to the surface as possible, though there is not too much to see of it."

John peered out through the eyes of his host at the planet growing bigger by the second, the alien working the spaceship by memory without needing to look.

On reaching Pluto, the alien reduced speed as he zipped the vessel through the ultra-thin atmosphere, levelling it up at five hundred feet and keeping it there.

As far as John could see, Pluto was a tiny, barren planet, with nothing but a rocky mountainous landscape; then he caught sight of something that changed his mind.

"Hey, what's that thing there?"

"That, John Philips, is a Kcraxxion space cruiser. It must have crashed landed there long, long before my race discovered the secrets of intergalactic travel," revealed the alien being somewhat matter of factly as they flew over what appeared to John to be a gigantic but derelict spaceship, half buried on the planet's surface below them. "Behold your possible lords and creators, John Philips, the tales of old tell of the Kcraxxion's visiting the third planet prior to setting off again into the stars."

John could only look down in stunned silence as his alien host told the tale of would-be Gods in the making, possibly nonsense but he listened anyway.

"It was told that the vessel developed a malfunction and that a team volunteered to remain on the third planet until a rescue crew returned; it never did."

Whatever the tale, it was still a breathtaking sight to behold as far as John was concerned. A massive monster of a spaceship never to see the stars again.

"Are you trying to tell me what I think you are here?" A furrow-browed John asked as they did a second orbit of Pluto, noting again just how cratered the planet actually was. Then he saw the crashed space cruiser again.

"That God himself may be lying dead inside that thing down there?"

"Not your God deity, John Philips, your creators would be a closer description. Legends tell of them terraforming entire planets in six of your Earth days."

John listened somewhat half-heartedly as his knowledgeable host continued with a tale he could only guess to be the truth; no one would ever know for certain anyway.

"The Kcraxxions were extremely technically gifted as well as being aware of time in a sub-atomic capacity, but now we must get you back on course for Earth."

On saying that, the alien pilot deftly altered course sending his vessel out of Pluto's orbit and out into space again, ending the lesson in the process.

"How many planets are there in our solar system, just nine or are there more?"

"There are seventeen planets altogether, John Philips, we've already journeyed three-quarters of the way through it skirting eight super giants en route to Pluto," volunteered his host as once again they headed for the distant star, the sun, still barely a flicker in the blackness of space all around them.

"The super giants are mostly invisible but give off very high-frequency micro-radio waves, making them near impossible to detect with the equipment your planet is using."

Neptune and Uranus were in turn big but uninteresting as far as John was concerned, all frozen oceans and crater-battered mountain ranges as they circled each one.

Saturn, once they reached it, was a different thing entirely with its magnificent rings of dust and ice, plus an array of over sixty moons, the biggest being Titan.

"Wow! Now that's what I call a planet," gushed a more than impressed John Philips, being the very first human being to gaze out on the planet; the ringed giant was almost touchable, they were so close to it.

"Yes, I agree, I too have a soft spot for axis-tilted worlds like the one you call Saturn, John Philips, it is the lightest planet in your entire solar system," informed the clever alien as they gazed at the magnificently ringed planet, a mostly gaseous, windswept giant, impossible to exist on but perhaps not its many moons. "The last time it was inhabited was by a species called 'Veeheapleaans' on the moon Titan, but I believe they have not survived and are now long extinct."

They sat gazing out on Saturn for a few more minutes, then the alien took them away heading to where his instruments told him they would rendezvous with the planet Jupiter.

Jupiter, once they approached it, was even more of the same as the vessel flew past several of its clusters of outer moons and began orbiting Ganymede, its largest moon.

"Oh wow! Isn't there supposed to be life on some of these bigger moons like this one?"

"Yes, John Philips, in fact, life exists on this very moon but not as you would readily identify. Also on lo, Calisto, Elara, and Europa, but then life is life, agreed?" The tri-pedal alien rumbled, hearing the goggle-eyed Earth boy mutter agreeance before continuing, turning its attention to the gigantic planet itself.

"As it happens, life does exist on Jupiter itself, enormous intelligent beings, like your planet's jellyfish, floating high in the unbearably destructive storm thermals."

Again, they sat taking in the incredible sights of both moons on one side and fantastically engaging planet overhead until the alien rather reluctantly broke orbit.

A few minutes later, all thoughts of Jupiter were momentarily ended as the alien steered his vessel into and through the frightening asteroid belt.

After several heart-stopping near misses, they continued for the last of their planet-hopping journey, with Mars the last one between them and Earth itself.

Mars, the so-called 'red planet', seemed to John to be one long, continuous dusty desert, dotted with mountain ranges and a twenty-two kilometre high volcano, Olympus Mons.

"Well, is there any life on Mars?" John asked as they locked into a reasonably low orbit and sat peering down at the rust-coloured planet below, both boy and alien enjoying the spectacle as one.

"I know that there is definitely life teaming away down there, not on Mars but deep under the surface. I have seen it for myself a long time ago," rattled off the confident-sounding alien as they flew over the deeply scarred canyon system called Vai les Marineris, the Grand Canyon but on a much larger scale.

"I do not know how to tell you this, John Philips, but the race of beings that live here do not want to meet their earth counterparts. Sorry, but it's a fact."

"I…I don't understand," was the only response John could proffer in the circumstances knowing nothing at all about Mars or of any people living on the planet either.

"Over one hundred of your Earth years ago, an astronomer saw canals containing water on the surface of Mars, from then on, it became what you see before you down there," drawled his extra-terrestrial host matter of factly, knowing that even though John was just a young Earth boy, the truth was still the truth, so he continued.

"They altered the molecular atom oscillations so that from that moment on, Mars would appear to be a lifeless, arid desert world, which is what you see now."

"Atom oscil…oscilla…why did they go and do that for?" A dumbfounded John Philips quizzed, the twelve year old Earthling child not understanding anything his alien host had just told him, hardly surprising in the circumstances.

"It means, my innocent young child, that they became all but invisible, dimensionally that is to those races they did not want to find them," was the reply from the alien expert piloting the starship. It was all strange as far as John could tell, surely all races could relate to other ones, or could they? "Do not get me wrong, John Philips, they are a peaceable race of beings, intellectually aware yet unbelievably shy, plus their wish for privacy is written into a cosmic treaty."

"Are you telling me that I can't see them yet they are there, anyway?"

"Yes, John Philips, that's exactly what I'm telling you. Even I cannot allow you to see them against that treaty. Oh, we had better be on our way, don't you think?"

"Yes, erm…how far is it to Earth from here?"

"A million miles from here in the direction of where the sun is right now, John Philips, our next destination." On saying that, the alien pilot peeled his vessel out of orbit and sped them away at frightening speed, leaving Mars far behind with Earth as their next port of call.

"Colonel Smithlington, I think you ought to take a look at my screen!" RAF technician, Susan Bartholomew, called gazing across at her suddenly attentive superior officer, a frown appearing on his face at yet another possible disappointment.

"What have you found, Susan? Not another anomaly I hope."

"No, not this time, Sir. It's our own friendly neighbourhood alien spaceship and it is heading our way," responded the equally unsmiling but ever-hopeful technician and RAF captain, quickly returning her eyes to the screen to see the tell-tale blip zipping through space.

"See that strong blip to the very left, I've been tracking it and it's travelled across our solar system like a hot knife through butter, stopping at all the planets in turn."

"Where? Show me!" An animated Colonel Smithlington gushed, having waited three long weeks, hoping upon hope that this moment would come along, and now it had.

"I calculate that it's doing much seventeen at the moment and it is heading straight for us on its present course," revealed the experienced, ever-dependable technician, aiming her dainty digit at the onscreen blip moving along at speeds they could only marvel at.

"Yes, that's our baby alright and it'll be heading to where it knows the boy's body is being kept alive," rattled off the glassy-eyed colonel, his mind already forming plans for them to get their first and lie in wait for it. It could mean promotion at long last.

"How long until it reaches Earth? That's supposing that it is our alien and not an altogether different one."

"By my calculations, it will be here in just under an hour. What do you want us to do, Sir?"

"I'll tell you exactly what we are going to do. Listen up because this time, there will be no escape from our illusive extra-terrestrial friend, none at all."

"I'm so, so sorry, Mister and Missus Philips, but we need both of your permissions to turn off the ventilation unit. John is technically dead," husked the grim-faced consulting specialist armed with the unenviable task of delivering bad news to already distraught family members, but someone had to do it.

"I know that sounds slightly indelicate but he is not displaying any brain waves at all, so we think it best for him and for you that we let him slip away."

"Oh please God, no! Surely there is something you can do that you haven't tried yet," bleated the boy's agonised father, tears not too far away from his red-rimmed eyes as he stood hugging his devastated wife, both having not slept for several nights in a row.

"We've done all we can. It's up to your son to do the rest and I am afraid that he is not responding. Sorry again but it is the right thing to do in the circumstances."

John's parents knew deep down that the consultant specialist was right in that their son might never return to them; John was at death's door.

"Can…can you give us a couple of minutes please to discuss things? It is an extremely difficult decision to make," sniffed the boy's trembling father, gripping his wife's hands tightly in his own, tears streaming down her face as she gazed helplessly at her son's lifeless body.

"Yes, yes, of course, take your time both of you. Believe me, it's for the best. See you in five minutes."

On saying that, the consultant turned and strode from the room with practiced respectful silence, allowing the grieving family to come to hopefully the correct decision on his return.

"Well, honey! What are we going to do? John is our son," ventured an unbelievably dour Roger Philips, his question not one he ever wanted to ask, only for circumstances to force the issue on them both.

"We…we ca…can't just let them turn his life off, can we?" A tear-drenched Gloria said, sniffing loudly up at her dour-expression-carrying husband, staring as if the answer was etched on his face only to see that it was anything but.

"He…he might come back to us at any moment, we can only hope and pray that he does for all our sakes," groaned Roger, his voice cracking with unashamed emotions as they stood together desperate for a miracle to happen and the stricken, lifeless boy recover for them.

"Wh…why doesn't he then? He is not going to, is he?" An emotionally drained Gloria Philips simpered; the devastated pair was desperate for John to give them a sign that he was still there and fighting for his life.

"We…we have to do what is right for our son as well as for ourselves here; maybe the doctor was right after all," proffered her pale, drawn husband, cradling his spouse whilst peering down at the boy they both loved very much but was not responding to treatment at all.

"Ro…Roger, no…no, we can't! We can't just end his life, he's our only son!"

"Gloria, let's face it, we might have to, for John's sake as well as our own; we have got to let him find peace and let him go."

Again, they hugged one another, this time tighter than ever as they stared somewhat tearfully down at their horizontal child. They had both made up their minds.

"Al…alright, you know I only want what's best for John. We will see him again, won't we, in heaven?"

Together, they stood weeping for their dead son lying in the iron lung keeping John artificially alive. It would soon end all hopes of his coming back to them.

For Roger and Gloria Philips, it was the worst day of their lives as the latter wept uncontrollably in her husband's arms and cried as well at the awful truth: 'John Philips was no more'.

"We are approaching your planet, John Philips, but we must be careful not to be noticed by Earth radar and risk getting shot down again," informed his alien host as the familiar blue and white planet called Earth suddenly shot into view up ahead, one moment a tiny dot the next a big beautiful world.

"Do you mean that it might not be safe for us to return to Earth after all?" A shocked John Philips exclaimed at the thought of them getting shot down and possibly killed before having the chance to see his parents again.

"Yes, that is precisely what I am saying. Your people will again attempt to reacquire my vessel and me by violent means, John Philips," confirmed the clever alien whilst busily resetting the panel or instruments, all totally incomprehensible to his passenger looking on.

"But I must get back again, mum and dad will miss me," blurted the worried-looking boy, his fears suddenly realised and instantly picked upon by his much more experienced host.

"Fear not, John Philips, I will not let you down. First, though, I must negotiate a safe pathway to take my vessel as close to the planet's surface as I dare," revealed his friendly alien tri-pede whilst simultaneously guiding the vessel into and through Earth's atmosphere, the walls solidifying to protect them from the heat friction. "They will no doubt be tracking us even in the darkness of the planet's night, but I have several tricks up my sleeve, as your species say."

"I only wish I could see and watch for myself what they do to try and shoot you down," droned John from within the extra-terrestrial's brain, hoping to be able to see for himself what the flying saucer they were in could do when under fire.

"If that is what you want, John Philips, let me deionise my vessel walls again and you can watch what happens."

On saying that, the alien pilot ran his huge right hand across the weird instrument panel and once again, the entire ship became invisible, allowing John an unrestricted view outside.

His enjoyment was short-lived as a glowing purple light to their left told the pilot that they were about to have company any moment now.

"They have found us, John Philips, forcing me to employ my big tactical diversion, one that should buy me enough time to get over to the area housing your physical body," announced the experienced alien having decided to put a plan into operation; one that he hoped would distract the humans closing in on him long enough to deposit the boy back into his own body again.

"Once your fighter jets have fired on us, I will fake a crash landing then utilise an external deionising device on the outer hull rendering us cloaked as you know it."

John did not reply or question his wiser alien pilot but peered out through his host's eyes watching as events unfolded out in the cloudy skies around them.

"You are about to take part in a serious time diversion, one, John Philips, that will be the envy of your fellow mankind if luck goes our way," his ET host informed him whilst keeping a close eye on one particular area of control panel and his right hand hovering over another sectional together.

"Relax and enjoy the spectacle as my technology outsmarts your own war-faring, antiquated flying machines with ease, with no casualties on either side hopefully."

On saying that, the cocky alien flicked its outstretched hand in a rolling motion as if attempting to catch an object thrown at it a moment earlier.

As John looked from within the clever alien's head, the entire spaceship juddered several times, pixelating in and out of focus for a moment, then returned to normality.

"There we go, John Philips, about to be shot at and then forced to the ground, but by then, you will be safely back into your own body and me out into the vastness of space."

"How? I don't think I know what you're talking about."

"Then allow me to enlighten you. I have despatched a replica version of this vessel, one with a limited life span going in the exact same direction as us," reeled off his preening host as they watched three tornado jet fighters zoom into view chasing the flying saucer they were supposedly inside, but were not. "They are unknowingly chasing a ghost. We, on the other hand, are rendered invisible and will soon be far away from here. Let's get you home again, shall we, John Philips?"

"Yes, yes, please!"

"Say that again, Flight Captain Stubbinton, say again?" A furrow-browed Colonel Smithlington quizzed after a moment's shocked hesitation, finding himself momentarily stunned and wanting to hear it again.

"We did as ordered, Colonel, chased and shot it down, only for it to melt away before our very eyes. I...I'm not sure that it was actually hit at all."

"What is on your radar right now, Flight Captain? Tell me what you see."

"Nothing at all close by, Sir. Hey! Wait a minute! There's a blip out on the coast twenty miles to the east of here. I think it's your UFO, Colonel!" A clearly surprised Flight Captain Stubbinton blurted, the experienced pilot hearing a verbal confirmation of the object from his trusted co-pilot in the seat behind.

"It's him alright. The bastard's trying to trick us again. Come and shoot it down, Captain, and that's an order."

"Yes, Colonel, we'll be right over; out!" The positive-sounding air force captain snapped whilst already indicating via hand gestures the intention for the trio to do just that.

"May I suggest you approach the UFO from three different directions in a pincer movement, that way it'll have nowhere to hide or fly to; go to it, group captain."

On saying that, an expectant Colonel Smithlington ended the call wondering why there was still no sign of it on their radar. Had it been his UFO or another one altogether?

"Where the hell is it? Anyone?" The disbelieving RAF officer exclaimed as the screen went blank taking the alien spaceship away with it, was it their equipment or something far more worrying?

"The equipment checks out, Colonel; either it's gone invisible or it's gone altogether," Susan reliably informed him as he gazed at the enormous wall-mounted screen, desperately attempting to locate the spaceship he knew was there somewhere.

"Invisible! Cloaked you mean? Oh, holy mother of God, no. If it is, then we will never capture it. Keep monitoring for it on all frequencies, we've got to locate it," boomed an anxious Colonel Smithlington as the screen remained empty of objects, only the approaching jet fighters way off to the right were visible.

"Colonel, we seem to have lost all contact with the UFO. What are your orders, Sir, over?" The leader of the trio of fighters volunteered about to enter the prearranged battle zone, only for their target to suddenly blink off on the radar.

"Continue course for the interception, Captain, fire at preset coordinates. You have a green for go, I repeat that is green for go. Good luck and out."

"Roger that, about to manoeuvre into attack mode. Enjoy the show, Colonel, out."

"I'm so sorry, Mister and Missus Philips, but your son John has gone to a much better place, up into the kingdom of heaven, or so they tell me," husked the dulcit tones of hospital chief consultant, Gillian Parstrum, having just that moment flicked the switch to turn their son's life support machine off.

"Do either of you want to say a few words about your dear offspring? You don't have to but you can if you so wish."

"Ye…yes. I would like to say goodbye to our son. It won't take too long but I need to do it and it's from both of us," spluttered a red-eyed, tearful Gloria Philips, who stood hugging her equally devastated husband as the noises from the machine began fading, then stopping altogether.

"Darling John, your father and me love, and will always love you. We will be with you in thought, so think of us now and again. Bye for now; sleep tight, our darling John."

Together, they wept openly in each other's arms as the iron lung gave a last gasp and then was silent, effectively ending the young boy's life in the process.

"I am deeply sorry for your sad loss. You can remain here for as long as you like, goodbye."

"Thank you, thanks for everything you've done, goodbye," bleated Roger Philips at the departing consultant, watching the woman walk away and then exit the room through tear-filled eyes before turning back to face his grieving wife.

They both knew that their son, John, had gone, cruelly taken from them by a twist of fate, one they had no influence over whatsoever.

Then Gloria saw something that made her jump.

"It is now time for you to depart. You have been a credit to your own race of bi-pedal beings and in my own way, I will miss you, John Philips," rattled off his alien host as they hovered invisibly over the hospital housing his own body, having outwitted those wanting to catch or destroy both him and his vessel.

"Do not be afraid, you will feel strong actions against your being. Do not fear or resist them, I am ready to engage soul transfer, prepare yourself and farewell."

"I…I've enjoyed myself in the main, seen some things no one else on my planet has ever seen, but it'll be good seeing mum and dad again when all is said and done," John admitted, more to himself than to his genial alien host, as he prepared for whatever came next, suddenly feeling giddy and nauseous somehow.

"Where will you go when you leave Earth? Back to that pleasure planet, you seemed to like so much?"

"No, at least not yet, but now you must get back to your family, home, and way of life, they will be pleased to have you there with them, will they not," volunteered the alien. He had begun to feel quite a friendship towards him, having shared minds and adventures with him; now though it was time to go home again.

"Remember to love, respect, honour, and obey those you do not wish to leave your circle of friendship. I have a feeling we will meet again sometime in the future. Farewell, my friend John Philips, farewell."

It was the very last thing he heard as everything suddenly pixilated, turning bright white before disappearing altogether in a frighteningly fierce jagged flash of lightning.

"M...Mum? Dad? I...I...I..." muttered a groggy John Philips, his barely audible words heard by his sobbing mother, Gloria, turning to gaze in the direction of her recently departed son.

"Mum, it's me, I made it back. I'm alive!"

"Jo...John? John! Ro...Roger, it's John! He...he's alive! John's back with us!" A wide-eyed Gloria Philips exclaimed, shock registering on her tear-smeared face as she slowly relaxed her grip and turned away from her equally furrow-browed husband.

"John! Oh my God! My baby has been sent back to me. John, you're alive! Roger, go and get a doctor or a nurse, quickly."

A bug-eyed Roger Philips stared at his beaming wife, then flicked his gaze to the visibly animated boy, then back to a pleading Gloria before heading for the door.

"Mum? Whe...where's dad going?" The pale, red-eyed boy bleated gazing at his rapidly departing father disappearing out of the door, leaving him alone with his shocked but relieved mother.

"He's gone to fetch a doctor! Oh, John, you frightened me. I...we thought that you had gone to heaven but you are here, back with us again," said his glassy-eyed mother, an unremovable smile on her dishevelled face, clearly over the moon with the situation she now found herself in.

"Forget him for now, how are you feeling? The doctor told us to turn the machine off. Sorry, my darling."

"I…I feel tired but fine, honest, mum. I need a hug. I'm so pleased to be back with you and dad," mumbled a grinning John Philips, having made it back into his own body just in the nick of time from the look of it as they hugged as only mother and child can do.

The next minute, all hell broke loose as his father rushed into the room followed a step behind by doctors and nurses, all eager to witness his miracle return to life.

John didn't care, why should he? He was back on Earth with his loving family Yes, the centre of attention. S question at the back of his mind he longed to have answered.

Had his friendly neighbourhood tri-pedal alien managed to evade those seeking to capture it or had the powers that be succeeded in shooting it down?

One thing he did know was that he needn't fear for such a clever, wise entity. It had made it and was away out into the depths of outer space, safely so.

It was all over, at least for him anyway. It was now time to carry on with his life back in the bosom of his family; but what an adventure.

With the human boy now back in his Earthly body, it was time to flee the dangers of the third planet escaping those clumsy machines attempting to destroy him and his vessel.

Once he had deactivated both the decoy and cloaking devices, he launched himself upwards at Mach five, almost colliding with one of the jets in the process.

"Whoa there! Bogey ascending at least Mach five. Anyone able to pursue, over?" The rattled pilot of the close encountered jet fighter exclaimed, quickly recovering his composure to see a blip rising at an unbelievable speed up into the clouds overhead.

"Colonel Smithlington here, I want one of you to get a shot away. I want that bastard shot down and that's an order," growled the miffed RAF officer-in-charge, staring up at the giant wall screen linked to the satellite peering down at the scene from space.

"Yes, Colonel, I'm heading towards it from the east so I should be able to get shots away before it exits the atmosphere. It'll be close but I'll do it I hope, over."

On saying that, the pilot yanked back the throttle and sent his jet fighter screaming skywards, fixing on than firing all he had at the departing flying saucer about to leave the atmosphere.

"Missiles away, target almost out of range, it's a no-go on impact, Sir. Bogey is now out in space. What are your orders, Sir?"

"Damn that alien! Okay, return to base and I'll let area command know the situation. Over and out," droned a suddenly crestfallen Colonel Smithlington, knowing full well that it was all over as far as capturing a UFO and its pilot was concerned.

With it went a reasonably distinguished career in the RAF as well having twice failed to ensnare the same spaceship, only to lose it both times.

As overall officer-in-charge of the operation, he must now face his direct superiors, who would no doubt post him to the British expeditionary base camp down in Antarctica.

It may well be time to rethink his career in the armed forces seeing as failure was scorned on by those higher up the chain of command. It was all over for him.

As far as the fleeing alien was concerned, the Earth boy John Philips would be sorely missed, mused the tri-pedal being setting a course for Rigel 6 and its binary twin planets.

There was no doubt that he was definitely a credit to his race of argumentative, war-mongering individuals, eager to learn but not to fight.

It was a pity that he wanted to return to the third planet, the two of them seemed compatible, yet the boy's instincts were unavoidably strong and trustworthy.

Fate would hopefully shine down on John Philips, that much he was able to deduce for himself as he left the solar system behind on his journey to Rigel 6.

Now though he was well on the way to the nine-moon planet, Waabraeakk, where he would spend plenty of time deageing amid the many mud canals sharing tales with others of his kind.

Once that was done, he fancied heading out to the uncharted reaches of space as yet not traversed by any of his own kind, somewhere unexplored and far from danger.

The future was far from fixed for some races of beings, thus it could be altered irrevocably by just one significant event, that may well have just taken place on Sol's third planet.

Perhaps John Philips had seen and learnt enough to one day aid humanity in reaching their dream to roam the cosmos as his race did.

Humanity, despite being an outward-looking, aggressively bloodthirsty, argumentative race of beings, was also clever, gregarious, and poetic people as well.

Hopefully, they would take the latter with them out into the stars; if not, then the intergalactic space council would not take kindly to them, not at all.

Failure to comply with their judgment spelt trouble in ways they could not imagine; the vastness of space had to be well overseen and protected at all times.

If they did decide to take anger and aggression out with them, they ran the risk of being 'time erased', destroyed by a deliberately placed black hole, a fate worse than death.

No one wanted that to happen, surely the uncountable number of galaxies and universes could be traversed in harmony and peace by all, as indeed did he.

Three months later, John Philips stood peering up at the sea of stars twinkling away through his bedroom window, his mind and thoughts elsewhere as his dad joined him there.

"It all looks so very big out there, doesn't it, John?" A star-gazing Roger Philips husked, himself no slouch when it came to amateur astronomy, having had a reasonably sized junior telescope when his son's age. Now he simply gazed skywards at odd intervals as John was right now.

"I longed to be amongst them myself when I was your age, had star charts on my bedroom walls, the lot. I even thought about becoming an astronaut once."

"Why didn't you then?" John asked without removing his eyes from the clear night sky, knowing that somewhere out there life was literally teaming whilst they remained stuck on Earth.

"I don't know. I suppose I never really tried to do anything about fulfilling my dreams; something I want you to do quite the opposite," revealed his equally engrossed father as they stood together, both seeking separate constellations in the blanket of bright heavenly bodies littering the darkness overhead.

"Follow your dreams, John, wherever life takes you and I promise that you'll reach the heights. The rest will be up to you, agreed?"

"An astronaut, that's what I want to be, Dad. I want to go up there and see the stars from the other side of the universe. I know it's there, Dad. I know, I've seen it myself," blurted the wild-eyed boy, hoping to be believed this time at least by his own father, turning to see the same expression of disbelief on his parents' face as everyone else he told.

"Of course, you have, son, or at least your mind told you the illusion that you did so. Remember what the psychoanalyst has told you, it's all in the mind."

With that said, he watched his smiling father turn and leave the bedroom, closing the door on a thoroughly disenchanted John Philips by the window.

Why would no one actually believe his story? True, it was highly unlikely and far-fetched; nevertheless it was a fact, he was not making it up.

Everyone he had spoken to about his planet and galaxy hopping with the genial alien had flicked their eyes heavenwards with utter alarm and disbelief.

People told him that he had hallucinated the entire episode due to the heady mix of drugs and imagination whilst comatose inside the powerful iron lung.

Now that all the fuss and excitement had died down, it gave him plenty of time for personal introspective thoughts as the occasional memory swept over him.

Was his true destiny really out there waiting for him to do what it took to reach out and grasp it? Hopefully yes, maybe the alien was right after all.

With Hornsea quickly back to normal, all gossip turned to the low-yield A bomb recently retrieved from the depths of the resort's freshwater lake.

With his father and mother having been made to sign the new Official Secrets Act, no talk of UFOs or aliens was spoken about by them or their son, John.

Three long months had passed yet the incident still haunted his dreams as well as most waking hours; his mind was blown away thanks to his impromptu space excursion.

As far as everyone else was concerned, everything was back to its usual dull self in and around the east coast resort as far as anything exciting was concerned.

The future for him was still a long, long way ahead and so was whatever lay in store for him, now though it was back to school and everything that it entailed.

He'd seen worlds and civilisations only dreamed about here on Earth. Surely that made him a special person, didn't it? Or was he simply the luckiest boy in the world?

Whichever one it turned out to be, he wanted more, lots more of the same. One day he would become an astronaut and see for himself the wonders of the cosmos.

Only time would tell if he'd make the grade…or not.

THE END